STATUE

IN THE

SQUARE

Joanne St.Clair

Statue in the Square

Copyright © 2010 by Joanne St.Clair

This book is dedicated to you. May you find happiness in all that you do and may you unleash the Spirit which is engraved on the inner chambers of your heart.

A Message from the Author

My journey to date has shown me that the true way to contentment, success, peace, joy, abundance and wellbeing, is by returning to the one source of Divine Mind and letting it direct us in our steps, Divine Mind being that which connects us all together and is the very life force of all that IS in life.

My journey has also taught me that few people dare to believe in this Divine Mind, maybe because it requires an adventurous and fearless Spirit and the possession of a mind which does not reason everything out.

I am both a witness to the workings of Divine Mind and a witness to the perils and plights of mankind. My expression in these pages is the middle ground which allows you to connect with that Mind which will solve every unsolvable thing, will achieve every unachievable thing, and will love every unlovable thing.

I write from a sense of duty to you, knowing that amidst the noise and banter of daily life, some of you will hear the whisperings of Divinity seeping through your very Being. When this happens, you will reach out and seek more understanding. This book is a part of your seeking and it is written so that you may understand more.

My sincerest thanks go to you, the reader, for providing me with a life so worthwhile.

Amen.

Joanne

March 2011

Contents

LIFE PLAN

Every gun makes its own tune.

The Good, The Bad, The Ugly

I wake in the night, sweating and panting, with nobody to soothe my fears or comfort me. It is just me, my quilt and memories of a haunted sleep. I turn and lie on my side, listening for creaks and groans of tired floor boards. The clock reads 3.33 a.m. It is too early to get out of bed, and too cold.

Moonlight peeks in through the window and casts its glow upon my face, bringing with it some solace. It pleases me that I am not lying here in total darkness because my mind may decide to play out its wicked tricks where I am made to envisage strangers creeping up the stairs, shape shifting in the darkened corners of the hallway and stooping low if I but dare to move.

I yawn and start thinking about how many hours there are until I must get up for work, deducing that if I rise at 7, I have nearly three and half hours of sleeping time left. When 7 a.m. comes around I have not slept, spending the past few hours caught in a grip of remembrance and being ruthlessly reminded of missed opportunities and subtle mistakes; of failed love affairs, bad reputations and silenced inner yearnings. At 4 a.m. I was somewhere between my childhood and womanhood, a place I regularly find myself, questioning how to make things – that is, my life – different. It doesn't require knowledge of rocket science to establish that the visions one has whilst asleep are inextricably linked to the experiences of our day. Therefore it's simple to assume that a recurring nightmare is a big hint that something in my life is not right. This is the third night in a row I've been the star of a Horror Movie dream.

Perhaps it has something to do with the frustration I am feeling in the workplace. I am not a violent person but recently I have felt hatred towards colleagues and the students whom I teach. Something inside of me dislikes them: I mean *really* dislikes them. Only the other day I imagined myself shooting some of them down and putting an end to their pitiful lives because they are doomed to failure anyway. The character in a story I read as a youngster administered death to the stray cats on the island of Corfu. Out of his desperate love for the feline beasts he decided it was better to pierce their heads with a single bullet than to see them scavenging for food.

I have the same feelings for my students, but it is not out of a deep love for them, it is because I do not feel as though I can stand it anymore. Systems, students, systems, students, each one playing the other, and within this mix are the teaching staff: my colleagues, on the continuous cycle of fiddling student pass rates to secure funding or, as one colleague puts it, moving goal posts to ensure the students complete their chosen course. Admission of students has got so poor that we are only one step away of asking the basic question of 'Can these students maintain their own body temperature? They can. Good. They *will* go to University and we will get them there!'

The thought of the workplace fills me with dread, and this dread has a habit of hanging around in my stomach like dry rot. How long can I go on like this? I am only twenty-seven years of age and yet I feel as old and run down as the colleagues who have served thirty years and counting. Is this the defining statement of my life: complete despondency and fear of tackling a normal day?

I look out of the window, gently pulling back the lace curtain which shields me from the outside world. A delivery van drops off daily newspapers at the convenience store opposite. Very soon money will exchange hands for this product, and millions of people will be discussing trivial details as though their whole welfare and social standing depended upon it. I shun these news topics, seeing them as a pollutant of my already fragile mind. I cannot understand why I would want to fill the cavity between my ears with tales of death and terror in unknown districts of the world when my life is filled with its own tragedy: that of going to work and conversing with people with whom I have nothing in common.

Three years ago, when I commenced employment at the college, I had vision. It felt as though I was destined for great things and would play a pivotal role in leading the Engineering department into the modern world. During the interview process the current Head of Department confirmed he was looking to employ someone with a high academic background who would take responsibility for motivating staff in the implementation of new technical courses. What he failed to tell me was that the actual roster of engineering staff was more concerned with pension plans and retirement benefits then they were any radical change, so their focus was to ensure that their jobs remained as easy as possible

This mental outlook soon became prevalent after only a few weeks in the role. Undeterred, I set about looking at ways we could work towards a more efficient department, in terms of improved paperwork and assessment plans. Each time a new way of working was suggested, every reason for opposing it was raised, with the majority attitude usually winning the day. 'Why do you bother?' my colleagues would say, 'Make it easy for yourself. Tick the right boxes, get your pay and don't kick up a fuss.'

With each passing day I felt, and feel, like the odd one out: a square peg in a round hole. Being the only female in the department further adds to my isolation. I am viewed as a hormone-ruled-being, someone who is erratic and emotional. Apparently all women are like this. But I think differently, knowing that this mismatch of attitudes is because my ideals don't match those of my colleagues. Their topics of conversation bore me: I see it all as doom and gloom and it is taking me into a world of despair and hopelessness. How long can I endure this, and why do I endure this?

I make the phone call and let the line manager know I won't be in today: I have had a bad night's sleep and I now have a headache. With an average absence rate of one day every four weeks, my excuses are running thin. It is with no doubt that I am jeopardizing my job – my reputation – but what will all this service to a futile entity amount to anyway?

I decide to phone mother for some consolation.

"Hello mum, it's me."

"Hello love. It's a bit early. I am just having a cup of tea. Can you give me a ring in twenty minutes?"

"OK. I just wanted someone to talk to."

"Let me drink my tea first then phone me back. I will talk with you then."

"OK."

"What time do you leave for work?"

"I'm not going today."

"Again! You'll lose that job if you're not careful. What's the matter now?"

"I told you I'm not happy there. Anyway I didn't sleep too well last night. I had a nightmare again."

"Well... tell me about it later. If I was you I'd get dressed and get yourself into work. Don't lose money if you don't need to. If I had my time again I'd be as hard faced as everyone else. They are only concerned about their money that lot! I tell you Jane, people are only concerned with money. Money and sex! And I bet that bunch you work with are gay. They are all probably sleeping with each other. They see you as a threat. That's what it is.........................."

"Look mum, I'm going to go. I might phone you later. I'm going to go back to bed."

"Ok love."

***

In the madness of life with its ups and downs, trivial concerns and nightmares, she doesn't change. She just sits in the same spot – day in, day out – glancing down and not making eye contact with any of the people that pass her by. I question whether her face looks serene or complacent, contemplative or lifeless. It is an answer I may never know but can only conclude that she is not affected by anything which happens in her immediate environment.

A child shares her seat and a second one maneuvers himself so that he is perched high on her shoulders. Nothing bothers her. Even when they try to move her she is resolute: sitting firm, immoveable. Behind her stands a small calf, also motionless, its face bent down as it chews the cud. But there is no cud: the ground is paved with brick. Not crazy paving, but neat, ordered, and acutely arranged.

A shawl drapes lazily over her shoulders and she holds it in place between the thumbs of her closed fists which sit neatly on her lap. Clogs peek out from underneath her ankle length skirt, and the seat upon which she sits looks like three folded woven blankets, one on top of the other, with a slight buckle where it supports her weight.

The children turn their attention to the calf. They straddle it and pretend to ride it, egging it on to *giddy up*. A parent sits nearby, absorbed in a cigarette and mobile phone, signifying the dying imagination of man. I tell myself that when I have children I will ride the animal with them, and we will imagine we are crossing wild rambling plains.

I am mesmerized by this young lady who occupies a small space in the Market Square. My name for her is the Statue in the Square, and when I need to get away to contemplate or to observe life, I come here to her. The mystery of this woman lifts my spirits. She is inanimate but her presence intrigues me. There is no knowledge of her deeds and yet she has left a legacy of mystery, like an unsolved case of crime. Someone, somewhere, knows the specific details. Could she at any point have been like me, just an average woman who discovered a method of escaping from the mundane of her life simply by watching people and observing their differing shapes, sizes, unique faces, hairstyles, skin colours and peculiar mannerisms?

This spot near the Statue is where I come to write, to note down my feelings and inner thoughts. My notebook understands and does not answer back –

my only true companion on this lonely road that I travel. Many times I have asked my notebook who the Statue was, where did she come from, and what did she do to be honoured in such a way? There is no accompanying information or plaque to commemorate her life. In fact there is nothing in the way of words. But this is not so bad. My granddad once told me that nothing can be a pretty-cool-hand.

Mother says that she has been dealt a bad hand. I retort but surely life is what we decide to make it. I try and raise this subject with educated professionals at work but their perspective is like mother's, confirming that your lot is your lot. Accept it and get on with it. I disagree because the comment from my granddad tells me that you *can* make something out of nothing.

Mother says I have to make the best of what I have already got, and warns that I am not to get too greedy or set my sights too high, that way I won't make stupid mistakes like her. She has been an idiot she reminds me. She says I should keep hold of a good job, pay into a pension fund and look after number one. They all say the same at work as well. What about dreams and passions I ask? Nobody has an answer for this, except in the way of a snigger, and then they change the subject and gossip about what other people are   doing.

A large grey cloud descends overhead, signaling the coming of rain. The temperature cools and the day darkens, making mid-day seem more like early evening. As the rain starts her downpour I decide to go to a café because there is no need for me to go home to an empty house to sit and mope about. In this vicinity I am comfortable in my exile, hiding out with no fear of seeing colleagues who may question me.

I scan the cafe for an empty table but it is lunchtime, so most are occupied. There are some vacant seats but I am limited in my choice, mainly between giggling ladies eating large slices of cake, and lone males in dark pin striped suits reading large newspapers. In today's world it is easy to give the appearance of being a successful man simply by dressing appropriately, which makes it difficult to tell whether one is a shop assistant, a doorman, a lawyer or a librarian.

This is one of the first points I noticed about Francois. The day we met he wore trousers which cost him three hundred pounds and a shirt which cost one hundred and twenty pound. He failed to pay this same attention to his underwear because he wore boxer shorts that were severely ripped at the seams. This lesson taught me much about people and how they like to give the impression of being more successful than what they are: all show and no substance. Image is one of the shallowest aspects on which we judge fellow man. We assume that if he dresses well then he *must* be successful. Oh! and how we hold onto the words of someone who we believe is blessed with success.

When I first started out in the professional world, I paid much attention to my image. Each day I wore clothes that I wouldn't normally wear because I convinced myself that if I looked the part, then I *was* the part. As I became more experienced I noticed that the majority of people in professional positions were not people I could aspire to, and I realized what a false ideal I was creating for myself. A man is more than his suit: this is just a prop to convey a role. When people say you can judge a man by his clothes, I reply 'maybe, but I have met many well dressed idiots.'

Now I look more like a student than a lecturer: jeans, well worn trainers, tight fitting jacket. My dress suffices for me, but not for mother. She tells me that my mode of dress won't attract a professional man. I tell her, 'mum, I don't want a professional man. I want a man who has a life, someone who makes me laugh.' She says 'Jane you can watch a comedy for a laugh, and socialize with people who have lives, but at the end of the day you need a man who can support himself. Take my word for it. I know!'

Mother is an authority on most subjects, and her mind is capable of working out problems without basic facts. Because she feels she has made many mistakes in her lifetime, she is frightened that I will do the same and so she tries to maneuver me in the directions she believes are most beneficial. I realize she does this out of love for me, but I ask which emotion is stronger: love for me, or fear for the mistakes she has made? There is a fine line between encouraging via love and stagnating via fear, but both can be clothed the same.

I carry my coffee to a vacant window seat. The table is occupied by a man who has his head in a book.

"Excuse me, do you mind if I sit here?" I ask.

He lifts his head from the book and looks at me. I wait for him to answer but he doesn't say a thing. As he looks I notice the blueness of his eyes. It is like looking into a glazier pool – a bottomless pond filled with crystal clear water. A strange feeling runs through my body and tingles run up my spine. This man must be over sixty years of age but his skin has the texture of a baby.

He smiles and replies, "Of course you may sit here. I have been waiting for you."

His response is strange. Perhaps he is a bit senile and thinks I am his granddaughter or something. He clears some space on the table and I thank him, placing my coffee cup down and then taking my coat off. As I do this I notice the title of his book, Universal Intelligence. At the side of his book are a pen and a pad with notes written on it. I decide not to take my writing pad out because I don't want to strike up a conversation. He may ask me what I write about, or he may want to talk of what he writes about. I decide to position myself on the chair so I am not sat directly facing him.

"Have you got enough room?"

"Yes, I am fine thanks."

"Good. Now we may begin," he says assertively. I look around the café for another vacant seat, but there are none. I try to avoid making eye contact so as not to encourage him, but he seems impartial to my show of uneasiness. I make an effort to control the situation.

"Excuse me...do I know you?" I ask.

He looks at me again, his eyes burrowing a hole through mine. I have never seen eyes like this before: they are alive and excited, full of laughter and peace, as if in wonder at everything.

"Yes, you do," he smiles.

I wait for him to elaborate but he says nothing more. I pick up my cup and drink from it, unsure of where to look. Does he know me or is he just saying this? His face is familiar but I don't recognize him. And those eyes! Surely I'd remembered eyes that are so striking. I sense he is reading my thoughts, intruding on my mental privacy.

"You allow people to enter your mind every day. They waltz in wearing dirty shoes, have a wander around and then they leave, without even having the courtesy to wipe their feet on your welcome mat, leaving you to clean up after them. The door to your mental palace is wide open at all times".

"I'm sorry but I think you've got the wrong person. I am not actually meeting anybody here."

"That's what you have assumed. But on this day you have been destined to meet with me. If you look closely, you will see it is in your Life Plan."

"My Life Plan?"

"Yes. Every soul that walks the Earth has a unique Life Plan. This Life Plan cannot be fulfilled by anybody else. It is assigned before birth: a *prerequisite* of birth to be more specific."

Mother always says that if she had a third leg she would kick herself up the backside with it, and this is how I feel now. It is just my luck on a day like today to choose to share a table with a crazy man. Perhaps I should have gone into work after all.

"Look, I am not sure who you are or who you think I am, but I have just come in here for a quiet coffee. I do not want to get involved in deep conversation."

"I know this but there comes a point in your life when you realize that things need to change. Unfortunately, like many other people, you are afraid of that change. The thing is, if you do not change you will never fulfill your Life Plan, and your life will have become a waste. You wouldn't want that would you?"

"Oh, and I take it that you are going to tell me how to make those changes?" I reply cynically, my patience starting to waver.

"I received an order two days ago to come to this town and on this day I was to wait for a person who fits your description. Here I am and here you are."

"An order? From who?"

"From the Giver Of Destiny," he replies, "more commonly known as G.O.D."

"Look, I think you have got the wrong person. Now if you'll excuse me."

I stand up and put my coat on, then pick up my coffee cup, deciding to move to a different place in the café. The person in front of me is talking like a mad man, about orders from G.O.D. and it is not what I need right now. My head is already bashed and I sense that if I encourage him he may attach himself to me. Also I do not have the time or the capacity in my life to open my ears to someone who is clearly deluded.

"You may walk away Jane Frasier, but I have been sent to give you instructions that will affect the outcome of your life. Walk away now and you will never know what they are. Stay and listen to what I have to say and you may claim the life that has been assigned to you."

He knows my full name. How does he know my

name? Who is this person? I turn and look at him. His piercing blue eyes are looking at me, peering out from a gentle face. There is no malice in his demeanor and he looks calm and kind, just how my granddad used to look.

He lifts his arm and motions for me to sit. Should I stay or go? Indecision hovers around my head. What is he going to tell me that can affect me so much? I am not happy with my life – that is certain. And it *is* rumoured that G.O.D. works in mysterious ways but there is no scientific evidence that G.O.D. actually exists. Perhaps this man saw my name written on something. But what? The last time I wore a label bearing my name was at junior school, and I have no credit cards in my purse with personal details on.

Then again, what have I got to lose? It will cost me nothing to give him an ear and as soon as I like I can get up and walk away. I glance around to see if anybody is looking at me. The café is still full and my cup is half filled with coffee. It is not like he can make any strange moves with all these people around. I decide to give him a chance.

"How do you know my name?" I ask, sitting back down.

"Like I said, I received an order to be here in this place at this time. You are my latest subject. I have a mission that I must complete."

"Just so you know, I don't believe in G.O.D. or anything like that. If you are trying to sell some sort of religion I am not interested, nor am I in a position to give you money. I am happy to sit here until I finish my coffee and then I will leave."

A smile spreads across his face.

"Let me introduce myself. I am Daryl Mason, a worker of the Light. Several years ago I gave my Spirit back to the Force that created me, and my life is now directed by that Force. I find myself in many situations such as this one and your reaction is nothing I have not encountered before. The mission I have been assigned in your case will last seven days, quite a long one compared to others. Sometimes I may simply deliver a message, other times I might act as a decoy to prevent a person from causing irrevocable damage."

"Seven days?" I repeat.

"Yes, that is correct."

Thoughts run through my mind, bringing with them images of abduction; of being beaten up and dumped in an alleyway somewhere; of being enticed to a religious lair somewhere in the middle of nowhere. The scenario fits in with many stories I have read: of chance meetings and missing persons.

"Don't worry. We will always meet in a place that is of your choosing, a public place, like here or somewhere else if you prefer, but we can discuss the finer details at the end of this session."

I look at him wide eyed, quite unsure of what to do and what to say. He seems to have everything figured out, as though he knows exactly what will happen over the next seven days and I am meant to just go along with it. What would mother say in this situation? She'd say 'Jane, don't be fooled by him. He is a con artist, that's what he is. Keep your purse closed and don't tell him what you do otherwise you'll never get rid. And if he is trying to convert you, tell him you're not interested. The Church of Looking-Out-For-Number-One, that's what we're about, Number One. And if that doesn't work, just tell him to............... '

"Ok, your Life Plan. I see here you are a Lecturer of Engineering, hmm, a technical mind. Always helps," interrupts Daryl. He looks at his notepad, reading from scribbled notes. "And you are obviously not happy with what you are doing otherwise I would not be here. What about the ending?" he muses, making brief eye contact with me, "now let me see." He turns a page and reads the text.

"What are you reading?" I ask.

"The outcome of your life, based upon one choice and two potential paths. Choose wisely and your life will reveal its magic and wonder. Choose foolishly and you will never unleash the wonderful potential and power of your Spirit. This is fatal and will lead to a living death during your lifetime."

A living death? Mother's voice speaks to me. It says 'Jane, drink your coffee and leave. Get yourself back to work.' I tell mother's voice to shut up! I am going to give this guy a chance. I have nothing to lose, and from what he is saying, everything to gain!

"Will you tell me more about this Life Plan?" I ask Daryl.

"The Life Plan is lesson number one, and is the first of our discussions. It is fairly straightforward and easy to grasp. Am I right to assume you have heard about   D.N.A?"

I nod, yes.

"Tell me what you know about it."

"I know that everybody has a unique D.N.A.

code and that people can be traced through their D.N.A. It acts as a map of the person, but I am not sure what sort of map. I think the codes correspond to factors such as eye colour and hair colour. Criminal investigations use D.N.A. samples and several weeks ago I watched a programme which traced people's country of origin through their D.N.A. I imagine D.N.A. to be a bit like a bar code that you get on products at the supermarket."

"You are on the right path Jane. The D.N.A. code is a highly intricate piece of data which stores everything that is related to one person. This code contains a persons' Life Plan. What is remarkable about this code is that certain pieces of it can only be accessed under specific conditions, hence why scientists have not yet discovered its full meaning. This specific condition is a connection to G.O.D. – the Giver of Destiny. G.O.D. is the Master Programmer of the D.N.A. code and only It – or He as I prefer to say when making reference to G.O.D. – has the language, the keys and the technical knowhow to unlock the secrets of the code. He would do, he wrote it."

He notices my face contort as I try to grasp what he is saying.

"Let me put it this way so you may understand the meaning of what I am saying. In this technological age, people throughout the world use computers on a daily basis. Some use them for basic functions such as writing a document or using the internet. Some people will use the computer to achieve more specific tasks, for example, accountancy, design, architecture. At the far end of the scale there are the actual computer programmers who compile complex programs of instruction that make these machines work. Unless you know how to understand and read the language that a computer program is written in, you will see nothing but jargon when you view it. If there are errors in the program, your computer malfunctions. Because you do not understand the programming language, you cannot repair it, and more often than not you need to seek technical assistance. This is no different to the D.N.A. code."

I understand what he is saying.

"So how does this relate to me and my D.N.A. code?"

"At the level you are operating at now, in your life as a whole, you are functioning as a front end user of the D.N.A. program: that is, you are only using its very basic functions. To fully master it and hence fulfill your Life Plan, you need to become familiar with its code and speak the language in which it is written. This is the language of G.O.D."

"I understand what you're saying about the language of the D.N.A. code, but how will this tie in with my Life Plan?"

"Embedded in each person's D.N.A. code is their Life Plan. This plan sets out their missions in life, missions that further the well being and happiness of mankind. When a person does not fulfill this Life Plan they become lost entities, like ships sailing through choppy waters without a captain. Because their life has been in vain, then their death will also be in vain. Their days will have been spent consuming resources – just eating, breathing and taking up space – without giving anything back. They will have left no legacy for the betterment of mankind and therefore cannot be remembered for their deeds."

Perhaps the Statue in the Square is a reminder of this basic fact: no name, no known deeds, just a solid object looking down at the ground as people walk by. Perhaps she and her calf are an analogy of the consumption: the calf eating all day, and both of them consuming space without any of them actually having any meaning or purpose for being in the Square.

"Are you saying that my life has been pre-arranged: that it is already set-out for me?"

"That is exactly what I am saying."

"So this frustration and apathy I feel about life is what has been laid down for me?"

"No. That is not the case. You are simply malfunctioning, in that you are not doing what you are programmed to do. You do not understand the language of G.O.D. and in this state you cannot fulfill the Life Plan which He has assigned to you."

"If this code - this D.N.A. code - that you are telling me about is linked to some higher purpose, then why have scientists not discovered it yet and learned to work with it?"

"That is a good question. Scientists want facts, and if they do not have facts, they theorise. Most scientists, although there are exceptions, don't believe in a Higher Power: an Intelligent Creator. They build their foundations on the Theory of Evolution – even though it is but a theory – and assume no knowledge and hence existence of G.O.D. Scientists are convinced that the Earth, and the people inhabiting the Earth, have come together out of chaos, out of another theory they have termed The Big Bang. But they fail to notice the acute order and system of things in the Universe."

I understand what Daryl is telling me. The science teachers at work deliver these theories to students on a daily basis. It is not ethically correct to teach about the possibility of G.O.D. but it is acceptable to teach theories such as the ones Daryl has mentioned. Only the other week I conversed with a physics teacher about the origin of life, and he was convinced in his argument that we had evolved from plankton or, to aid student understanding, fish. Later in the day, after this conversation, I relayed the discussion to an engineering tutor who was adamant that the basis of the Theory of Evolution was seriously flawed because the carbon dating methods that were used in science were highly inaccurate. The tutor had worked in the nuclear power industry and much of his work involved studying the decay of atoms. Apparently, carbon dating is flawed because the carbon atoms do not decay in a linear method as scientists assume: they follow a curved path, and therefore the Earth is not even half as old as pushers of the Big Bang theory believe.

Daryl continues. "Because most scientists don't

believe in G.O.D. they do not know how to access some very vital parts of the D.N.A. code. You could tell them until they were blue in the face but, unless they believe in a Master Programmer, they will never obtain the answers for which they search. They will continue chasing their tails in the quest for facts, facts and more facts, and if they cannot find facts they will create theories and pass them off as fact. I call it scientific propaganda! Only the true scientists of life will find the answers, like Einstein."

Daryl nods his head as if checking that I am still following him. I nod back so he continues speaking.

"Einstein believed in the existence of G.O.D. and made it a purpose to understand G.O.D.'s thoughts. To do this he must have been conversant in G.O.D.'s language and it is this which gave him the breakthroughs he searched for. Einstein unlocked his D.N.A. code and fulfilled his Life Plan. If only other scientists would follow his lead."

Daryl shakes his head, showing this is one of his frustrations in life.

"If what you are saying is correct," I respond, "it seems that everyone has the potential to be a genius, to do great and wonderful things with their life, if only they accept the destiny – the Life Plan – they have been given."

"Of course! That is exactly what I am saying."

What he is telling me doesn't make sense. If this is correct, why are so many people disappointed with their life and why do the majority refuse to even acknowledge the possibility of a Master Programmer freely giving out individual destiny's in life? Mother, work colleagues, friends and even their parents, all complain about their life. They are readily willing to tell me about the mistakes they have made in life, how they are not one of the lucky few who are given success, and that all they can do now is make the best of what time they have left in life. They are convinced this is how it is for everybody except a chosen few, and in their eyes the chosen few are people that I will never meet or ever be like, as though these few exist in a place which is out of reach to people like me. Daryl reads my thoughts.

"The people you are thinking about – the masses as I call them – will live mundane lives because they choose it for themselves. Those few that seem *lucky* enough to be *given* a happy life were not given it at all. They made crucial decisions and they chose their life. Luck signifies chance, but the Universe is supremely ordered. It is based on a series of fundamental principles which are available for everyone to work with, like the Law of Gravity, or the Law of Electricity. Life is not based on the outcome of a rolled dice."

"They *chose* their life. How?"

"At some point in everybody's life they will get the Call – just as what you are getting now. The Call is a known point in time when somebody appears and gives them an option, or they may have a feeling so powerful that they need to do something drastic. They may even have a simple thought that consumes their mind, pushing them to act on the thought even though it is completely foreign to what they know and it goes against all of their man made logic. This is the Call of G.O.D. and it is the moment He steps forward to offer a person their destiny. Because of doubt, fear, and many other excuses, most people seek to ignore the Call. When this happens, G.O.D. leaves them to their own devices until they decide, if they ever *do* decide, to seek Him."

"Does the Call unlock the D.N.A. code?"

"Yes, that is correct."

"So are you here to tell me my Call?"

"No. I am here to teach you a series of lessons which will show you how to speak the language of G.O.D. and enable you to heed the Call when it comes. You have a special role to fulfill and it is important that you make the correct choice."

I take a sip of my coffee whilst Daryl opens his notebook and picks up his pen.

"My work for today has been done. We will meet tomorrow and in the meantime I ask you to think about the role models in your life," he says.

"But I have to work tomorrow. I cannot take another day off!" I protest.

"The choice is yours. I will be here at eleven a.m. and will wait for thirty minutes only. Goodbye Jane."

***

During the bus ride home my mind sways between excitement and dread. I have never before met a stranger in a café who has spoken of such matters as Life Plans and D.N.A. codes. At work I am always preaching to students about the importance of having plans and timetables and many times I have had discussions with colleagues about the purpose of life. Ian, a 44-year-old electronics teacher, is adamant that the purpose of his life is to drink as many pints of beer on Friday and Saturday night's as is possible. 'But surely there has to be more to life than that,' I say to Ian. 'Jane,' he says, 'you take life too seriously. You ought to lighten up.'

The bus halts to collect passengers and I see Mick, a person I used to socialize with. He comes and sits next to me.

"What have you been up to?" he asks. "I have not seen you in ages."

I tell him about the conversation I have just had with Daryl but he seems not to hear me. At the first opportune moment he interrupts and proceeds to tell me about his recent weekend. He says he went to a super-club in Manchester and took a drug that, until recently, was only used in psychiatric hospitals.

"It is called the Simeon Effect," he says proudly, and then tells me that he took one dose of it and danced all night. He was high until Sunday night and didn't think he was ever going to come down. It was the best trip he has ever done and it only cost twenty-five quid. "Do you want me to get some for you because I am on my way to buy more now?"

"No thanks Mick, I am not doing that stuff anymore," I reply.

"It's your loss," he tells me. "If you change your mind just give me a bell. Anyway, it was good to see you but the next stop is my stop." He stands and starts walking to the front of the bus.

"Yeah, see ya Mick."

***

I arrive home still thinking about my meeting with Daryl. I wonder what his background is and whether I am being foolish by getting excited at what he had said to me. His words give me a feeling of adventure, like Indiana Jones on a mission to save a vital piece of history. Daryl said he was going to teach me a series of lessons that would allow me to hear the Call. Does this mean that I have been singled out for some great works? Surely not! It is me, Jane, from a terraced house in Blackpool, the pit of the North of England. I phone mother.

"Hiyah Mum. It's me."

"Hiyah love. Are you feeling better?"

"Yes. I went into town and had a strange experience."

"Yes. I had a strange experience today as well. The bus driver tried to charge me extra money but I told him he was wrong. As you know, I always pay sixty-three pence when I travel from town. We had a few words so I threatened to complain, then he apologized and said he realized his error."

"Oh..... ."

"Anyway, I bought myself two lamb chops from the butchers and I thought I'd have them for my dinner with some new potatoes and peas. What are you having for your dinner love?"

"A bit of Life Plan with a side serving of D.N.A.!" I reply.

"What? Are you alright?"

"Do you want to hear about my day mum? Something quite strange happened to me today."

I tell mother about the meeting with Daryl. She advises that I should not meet him tomorrow but must go into work. I ask her what she thinks about destiny, and G.O.D. She says it is a fool's game and doesn't pay the bills.

"Anyway, who was this man and where did he come from?" she enquires.

I tell her that he was directed by G.O.D. and that he is to assist me as part of his mission. She asks me if I am totally stupid and can I not see the writing on the wall.

"What writing?"

She replies the one which says I am an easy ticket to the bank. "Men can spot intelligent women Jane! He is good at his game."

"But I found what he was saying to be quite fascinating. For the first time in a long time I actually feel excited about something. He asked me to think about my role models in life. Nobody has ever encouraged me to do that before."

"Look love, I don't know where your head is at the moment but whatever you do don't jeopardise your job. Have you not thought he could be from the college, trying to catch you out so they can suspend you? After all, you *are* a threat to that lot there you know."

My heart sinks and I feel low. Before I spoke with mother I felt great, but now I just want to crawl up in bed and hide. The conversation with Daryl was a bit *out there*, possibly *too* out there to have any real meaning. If I told my colleagues about it they would laugh and ask if I had been drinking or, more so, if the old man Daryl had been drinking. My friends would say that I have been smoking too much marijuana. Then a voice from inside asks, what does your *heart* say and how do *you* feel?

***

The full force of the sun beats down upon my face. It is so strong I can hear it pulsating. My lips are dry, crisp, and the skin around my eyes is burnt, as though a red hot poker has been inserted into my sockets. Sand filled cracks, from where I have been pushed head first into the desert ground, seep from my lips at all angles.

A scorpion runs past me, on a journey to an unknown destination and oblivious to my peril. The maracas of a rattle snakes tail can be heard, this odd musical sound filling every last bit of breathable air. Over me stands a man with a shot gun.

"At least give me some water," I plead, my voice husk and grave. He holds the gun in front of me, a few feet away from my head.

"A foolish man always waits until he is dying of thirst before he quenches it. In the abundance of water he is thirsty...."

"I don't need a lecture. I am aware of my mistakes!"

"When confronted with death, the errors become apparent," he says.

He kicks sand into my face. It sticks to my skin but I am unable to move the grains because my hands are tied, tight.

"Just give me some water," I yell in a barely audible tone. "You treat me as though my life has no value to you."

"You live in a world where life has no value, or have you not realized?" I do not answer. "When this is the case," he continues, "death carries a price."

His whole figure is but a large black object, a solid shadow against the blazing sun. I squint to see his face but can see no features – no details – just the outline of a hat and the gun which is held in his hand and pointing directly at me.

"What do you want with me?"

"I want nothing from you, only the financial reward. This is nothing personal. It's just a job. You have spent your life working for money even though you have not enjoyed the manner in which you have earned it. We are the same, you and I. There is no need to feel like a martyr. We all sell our souls, in one way or another. You are just another face whose life is about to come to an end. I see myself as administering the full stop which will finally eliminate your sorry existence."

He thrusts the double barrel into my forehead.

"Adios sucker," he says, and slowly pulls back the trigger.

I wake and my body is drenched with sweat. My heart beats fast – boom, boom, boom, boom, boom – a time bomb in my chest waiting to explode. My mind races over the nightmare scanning for fragments of images, hoping to piece it together in a quest to understand what it was all about. The clock reads 4.08 a.m. - its red digital numbers penetrating the chilled air in the dark room, and I hear the tap, tap, tap of water dripping against porcelain in the bathroom.

EGO-SELF and TRUE-SELF

Beneath the make-up and behind the smile, I am just a girl who wishes for the world.

Marilyn Monroe

It is quarter past eleven and I walk at a fast pace towards the café. The town centre is busy and the bus was delayed. I have hardly slept and it shows in the dark rings under my eyes. I feel like breaking down and crying but this won't solve anything. The stranger has given me a life line and, even though it appears I am being foolish, it is my only option at this moment in time.

He sits in the same place as yesterday and his head is down, immersed in a book. A sigh of relief leaves my lungs and a smile spreads across my face. He notices me as I enter, and he waves at me. He looks as though he is pleased to see me. As I approach the table he stands, greeting me like I am an old friend. My feelings of fear melt away.

"I am glad you decided to come Jane, although I was confident you would. Can I get you a coffee?"

I settle into a seat whilst he is at the counter. His book, Universal Intelligence, lies on the table so I pick it up and open it at a random page. A sentence stands out at me. It says *What you do instead of your work is the real work.*

Daryl returns and places a cup of coffee in front of me. He sits down and leans on the table, his attention firmly focused on me.

"Yesterday I asked you to think about your role models. Have you done this?" he asks.

I tell him I have, taking a piece of paper from my bag and placing it on the table.

"Today we are going to look at your inner qualities. Hidden inside of you are some very special assets that need to come to the fore of your character, because it is these assets which will allow you to fulfill your Life Plan. At the moment your life is lived from qualities which are detrimental to your True-Self, and so we will also look at these and then determine how we can begin to eliminate them."

"I don't quite understand. I am not sure I can be any different."

"Oh yes you can. And this is our second lesson, the lesson of *Ego-Self* and *True-Self.* "

"Ego?" I reply, unsure of what he is getting at. I don't see myself as having any ego. I am not a person who walks around in love with myself, showing off to the world and acting as though I am the best thing on two legs.

"Yes, Ego! To be at peace with ourselves we need to know ourselves, and only when the Ego-Self has been banished will you see and understand the real you. Let me give you a definition."

Daryl opens his book and reads from it.

"*Ego: The conscious mind based on the perception of the environment from birth onwards.* So, you see, everything you *think* you are is nothing more than what you have seen and experienced in your environment. This does not mean that you are the True you, the person you are capable of being."

He sees the look of confusion on my face.

"Imagine you were brought up in another country, another era, with different people. Do you think you would still be the same person?"

"No," I answer immediately.

"Correct. But one thing *would* be the same, and that is the inner self: the True-Self. Think back to yesterday. What did we talk about?"

"We talked about D.N.A. and Life Plans, and you told me that we are programmed before birth."

"So what conclusion can you draw?"

"If we are programmed, it means we are also a certain way, and that our personality is decided before we are born," I reply, looking to Daryl for confirmation that I have given him the correct response.

"Our Spirit is programmed; our personality is not. The Spirit is the Force that drives your life, and the personality is the façade that you show to the world on a daily basis. A personality based life lacks depth and leads people into situations of turmoil and despair. A Spirit driven life leads to peace and happiness, and this is the birthright of every human on the face of the Earth."

A breath of excitement gets caught in my lungs. I have only been in the strangers company for fifteen minutes and already I feel uplifted, as though I am going to receive a revelation that will change my life. I feel good and strong. He reads my mind.

"The Truth will set you free Jane. But that is another lesson. Today we need to get to the bottom of your personality so we may reveal the Spirit that is trapped inside that shell of yours," he says, pointing to my body.

I see the twinkle in his eyes and notice that they are green today. Yesterday they were blue. They look as though they have been painted in Technicolor: drawn onto his face and shaded in. His eyes remind me of the bright colours I used to see in films when I was a child, bringing back memories of Charlie and his golden ticket to the Chocolate Factory, a ticket which gave him access to a world of fantasy. When Wonka opened the door to his secret world, he sang a song and part of it said,

If you want to view paradise, simply look around and view it.
Anything you want to do, do it.
Want to change the world, there's nothing to it.

If only life was this easy.

"Oh, but it is." Daryl's voice interrupts my thoughts. "Tell me about your role models Jane. Who do you most admire, and for what reason?"

I look down at the list on my paper and suddenly feel conscious about revealing the names I have written down. There is nothing to lose, I remind myself, and because he is a stranger I can walk away at any time.

"The Man with No Name, from Sergio Leone's Spaghetti Western films."

Daryl writes this down on his notepad. "Anymore?"

"Yes, I have several more."

"Ok, you read them out then we will come back to each individual and look at what it tells us about *you*."

"Marilyn Monroe, Nelson Mandela, Jean D'Arc, and Catherine Cookson."

"Good, now let's start with The Man with No Name. What do you respect or admire about him, and why have you chosen him as a role model?"

I was not expecting him to probe so deep and had not given this any previous thought. I sip on my coffee, taking a few minutes to think. Daryl watches me but I do not feel rushed. In his company it is as if time stands still and there is no pressure to do anything hastily.

"He always keeps a cool head and rarely speaks, and when he does his words have so much meaning. It also seems that he is not fazed by any situation – even if it is life threatening – because he has a confidence about him that makes even the toughest of men feel inadequate. Sometimes you don't know whether he is good or bad, because he doesn't side with either, he just does his own thing. He will play the bad guys off against each other so that they bring about their own destruction."

Daryl writes on his note pad and then motions for me to continue. "Ok, and the next one, Marilyn Monroe."

"Well she is, was, very attractive, but in her sexual prowess she also seemed vulnerable. She reminds me of somebody who craved a great love but this is, I suppose, a weakness and not strength. Perhaps she was foolish. My mother says only fools believe in love. " I feel my cheeks going red. Have I have revealed a bit too much about myself? Mother's voice says 'Be careful what you say. People will take advantage of you!'

Daryl notices. "It's OK, nothing to be ashamed of. Carry on."

"I think people took Marilyn Monroe the wrong way, and based all their perceptions on her image, but I imagine that deep down she was a very intelligent woman." Daryl does not need to tell me that this statement resonates with me: I know it does. I am aware of how ill judged I am and how my career to date has been a constant quest to prove myself in the eyes of male colleagues.

"Marilyn is one of the few women who I find beautiful because there is something so very sincere and womanly about her."

"And what do you find inspiring about Nelson Mandela?" he asks.

"The way he sat patiently for twenty-three years, holding true to his beliefs and always living in hope at a better way of life for him and others. As a child he wanted to run through fields without being threatened with a gun. As a man he wanted to walk on the paved streets, to be treated as a human being. Because of this he gave his life to a cause and in the end, he won. His story has inspired millions of people throughout the world and I admire his strength and determination. When Nelson Mandela smiles his whole face lights up and you can see that he has found peace and happiness, and that he does not carry bitterness for the years he endured in prison. In his quest for freedom he was subject to confinement, but in the end he secured freedom not just for himself but for the peoples of his nation."

I surprise myself at the words coming forth. If I didn't know it was me I would think that somebody else was doing the talking. It feels good and I could have conversations like this every day, but for some reason I rarely meet people who are interested in such subjects. This is why I befriend the pen: it allows me to share my inner thoughts with nobody but myself, whilst at the same time granting me the freedom to air my feelings. I could spend every waking hour simply writing and observing life, and then sharing my experiences with anonymous readers. Poems, short stories and part finished novels sit in a drawer in my bedroom – a documentation of the life of a nobody thus lived so far. For a moment I forget that Daryl is sat facing me, waiting for me to continue speaking. I look at my notepad.

"Jean D'Arc," I say. "She is the ultimate super hero in my eyes." I feel my cheeks go red again. Daryl makes humour of the situation and asks, "What, greater than Superman?"

"Give me Jean D'Arc any day," I reply light heartedly. "She is the true warrior, the finest example of how gutsy a woman can be. At seventeen she led the armies of France to victory. She had no military training; was uneducated and illiterate and yet she achieved in months what an army of trained experts failed to do in nearly one hundred years."

"Jean D'Arc is a favourite of mine too. I am glad that you have mentioned her because we will use her tactics as an example in one of the forthcoming lessons." Daryl looks at his watch. "Do you have any more?"

"Yes, one more. Catherine Cookson."

"Interesting! I have not come across that one before. How do you relate to Catherine Cookson?"

"I don't know how I relate to her, but I admire the fact that she wrote over one hundred books, and she did not start writing until the age of fifty. Her books touched millions of people worldwide." I do not tell Daryl that what caused her to write was the desire to free the pain that was trapped inside of her, and it is this which truly inspires me. Catherine Cookson spent her life feeling inadequate, as though she never fitted in anywhere; always carrying the stigma of being an illegitimate child. When her husband was feared dead in the war, all those years of stifled emotions surfaced, and her choice was either death by suicide or to simply let them all go. She chose the latter and released these pent up feelings by writing fiction, becoming one of the most renowned authors of the day.

Many days I feel like this, as if I cannot contain the emotions that linger inside of me. I envisage myself boarding a plane to an unknown destination, carrying a small hold all, a notepad, a pen, and a cloak of passion for the written word. But this is not a reality: it is fantasy! Who will cover the mortgage? How will I fund the trip? And more so, what will mother say? Daryl looks at his watch again.

"It is time for me to go now. We have come to the end of today's lesson."

I am confused. He has not taught me anything. All I have done is told him who my role models are. Why is he leaving me now? What good has this meeting been?

"I don't understand. You said that you were going to teach me how to look at my qualities and you would show me how to differentiate between the Ego-Self and the True-Self. I don't get it. It feels like we have only just started!"

"Look," he says, "all the answers you need are already inside of you."

Daryl tears the paper off the notepad he has been writing on, folds it and places it in my hand.

"Look in the mirror when you get home and ask yourself what do you see? On that piece of paper is a summary of what you have told me today. Read it. Analyse it. And understand it. I will meet you again, same time, same place, tomorrow."

"But......."

"No but's. Trust me."

I watch as Daryl exits the café. I was not expecting this and find myself questioning if I have done something to offend him. But he doesn't seem like someone who would take offence. Did I take too long in telling him who my role models are? I too leave the café and walk towards my place of solace, the area in the Market Square where I am anonymous and nobody knows what is going through my mind.

I sit facing the Statue with the piece of paper still in my hand. Since Daryl's quick departure a feeling of disappointment has engulfed me. He told me *we* were going to look at my inner qualities, analyse them, and then determine which ones were of the Ego-Self and which were of the True-Self. I have never looked at my character in this way before. Surely I can't do this on my own! But what did he say? He said that the answers are already within me.

Two days ago I did not know this man. He walked into my life and started talking about Life Plans. He said everybody had a Life Plan: it was part of an individuals' D.N.A. code. Then he told me he was preparing me for the Call and that he was going to teach me a series of lessons that would enable me to respond to this Call, which in turn would enable me to fulfill my Life Plan - a unique destiny assigned to me by G.O.D. The Call can be in the form of an urge, a feeling, an inner knowing, a chance meeting - it could basically come in any form and I had to be ready for it when it came. To be ready for it, I need to be able to speak the language of G.O.D. Many people ignore their individual Call because they are frightened of the consequences, or they do not have the courage to change their current course of action. He said that I was to choose wisely because the people that ignore their Call usually live a life which is not fulfilling, or to be more specific, a life which becomes a living death.

I know a lot of people like this, especially my work colleagues. Perhaps they always come to mind because my life is spent in close proximity to them -

Monday to Friday, 9 to 5. They are an excusable lot in that they base their life on excuses and the fact it is usually everybody else's fault. They live their life in a reactive way: a way which only acts when a problem presents itself. They believe they are at the mercy of life, and worry at the thought of anything suddenly changing their current situation. This type of life is a life of 'what if': what if I lose my job, what if pension regulations change, what if the department undergoes a reshuffle. This attitude means that they are controlled by the potential actions of others, making them nothing more than leaves being tossed about in the wind.

The Statue still looks down at the ground, reluctant to make eye contact with me. The role models I spoke to Daryl about are my ideals in life, but in reality I am closer in form to the Statue than I am any of the people on my list. Who knows, she may be holding a piece of paper in her clenched fist, unable to look at its contents for fear of being required to make a decision. Perhaps this was when she turned to stone – hard, cold, unmoving. Is she really alive on the inside, but dead on the outside, cast into a shape that even the seasons cannot alter? Could this be my fate if I fail to heed the Call, the moment when G.O.D. – the Giver Of Destiny – steps forward with my golden ticket?

Am I really so foolish to think that I may have potential in me as great as some of the wonderful minds who have achieved remarkable feats for mankind? I hear Daryl's voice: 'You must choose wisely and let the Force that created your Spirit drive your life.' Mother's voice interrupts him, and says, 'Don't you go filling your head with fantasies. You have a good job Jane and mustn't jeopardise it. Let somebody else go chasing after destinies, somebody who doesn't have as much to lose!'

People walk past in all directions, scuttling in and out of shops, carrying purchases in plastic bags. Some people look weary, downtrodden, as if they have had enough of life and are now going through the basic motions. The only real life on the Market Square is that from children, running around and calling out, oblivious to the pressures of adult life. I imagine what it must be like to have the eyes and attitude of a child for my whole life, always looking out and seeing adventure and fun. Is this a realistic way of spending the time I have on Earth? Because few people do this, does it mean it cannot be done? Imagine if Jean D'Arc and many others listened to the voice that said *it cannot be done*. Where would their legacy be now I wonder? Can I really choose the life I so desire, that which cries out to me from the recesses of my heart? I tell myself it starts by opening the paper that is nestled into my closed hand. It starts now. The adventure has already begun.

As if un-wrapping a single sweet, I slowly peel back the folds in the paper. In Daryl's neat handwriting I see five words:

Confidence

Sensitivity

Freedom

Warrior

Accomplishment.

Underneath the words, it reads

Look in the mirror – what do you see?

***

As I look in the large mirror I see a person who is unhappy: frustrated with her life. I see stress lines under the eyes: dark rings which start from the corners of the eye and run outwards over the top of the cheek.

The words on the paper come to mind. To onlookers I appear confident, because I am outgoing and laugh a lot, but inside I feel afraid. Like Marilyn Monroe, I am all too ready to fall in love, and this at times has proved unfulfilling, causing me hurt and sadness. I am also sensitive to other people and their needs as I genuinely care for people. This is why thoughts of shooting my students give me cause for concern and I know, within, that it is a cry for freedom, but the freedom I crave is a mental freedom, that which gives me the choices of living the life I envision when I sit alone daydreaming.

As a child I would seek revenge on the bullies at school and fight for what I believed was right. Their behaviour of tormenting and hurting innocent bystanders disgusted me, and I felt a duty to care for those who appeared vulnerable and unable to defend themselves. Perhaps this is the warrior in me and is what resonates with Jean D'Arc.

Then there is accomplishment. I do enjoy achieving but even this has lost some of its steam over recent years. My enthusiasm for achieving in a job which brings me no satisfaction has faded. I ask myself what is the point of climbing the career ladder if it is leaning against the wrong wall? These are the assumptions I make as I stand looking at myself, but a small voice tells me to look deeper, to see below the surface.

I stare hard at the eyes looking back at me, and slowly my face starts to blur. It feels as though I am journeying inwards, toward the center of my being. I see fear and loss, and it reminds me of a wild horse that has been held captive until its spirit has broken down, given up, long forgotten its desire for freedom. I imagine breaking its chains and encouraging it to run, run, run away; to go and run with the wind, to gallop across open fields, to feel the pure spirit of life pumping through its veins, carrying power to every muscle.

I imagine myself leading an army of people who are all searching for the life that once ran through their blood and gave joy to their hearts. They see me as their refuge and their hope, and they know that I care for them. My belief in G.O.D. and the confidence in His ways are so strong that these people feel empowered in my presence and are able to see an escape from the mortal gloom of their foolish choices.

Standing at the head of the convoy, I speak to the people. Some onlookers try to belittle me, to discourage our fight for a better way, but my words cannot be beaten. I am cool and collected, with an answer of maximum impact for every comment that I hear. This stirs up the people before me and their Spirits lift higher. We feel so confident that any man who disagrees with our plight no longer dare say so, because he is no match for the few words which come from my mouth. I am able to play the good against the bad, and the latter literally shoot themselves down with their own ignorance. We stand mighty and firm as I, one person, inspire courage and confidence in the masses.

I am beginning to understand what Daryl is conveying when he talks of Ego-Self and True-Self. The Ego-Self is the charade that I act out on a daily basis, a personality whom I think I should be. Wearing a mask of professionalism, I go to a job that offers no real fulfillment because I *think* it is what I *should* be doing during this stage of my life. The Ego-Self is she who hides my real passions and beliefs and thoughts because she is frightened of people thinking I am weird and abnormal. This side of me harbours fears, and the key is to understand where these fears originate from and what I can do to overcome them.

I am twenty-seven years of age and I see I have been caught between two worlds; two states. There is the side of me, the True-Self, who lives in hope at life and dreams of greater things; and then there is the Ego-Self which is frightened to step outside the norm in case failure rears its head and bites at my ankles, causing me to stumble to the ground where it can wrap itself around me and squeeze every last drop of life out of me.

And now Daryl has come into my life to teach me how to recognize my Call. I am aware that I have only one chance at life and inside I know I must live it as I choose. Just the thought of spending the rest of my working days at the college makes my stomach churn. Dave, a colleague, reminds me that *he* said he was leaving the job twenty-years ago but he is still there. Derek says 'before you know it Jane time has gone and it is too late to move anywhere.' I say to Derek that surely nothing is ever too late, and he says, 'you'll see. It is not as simple as that. Just you wait until you get a mortgage and a family. There are commitments that you must fulfill Jane.'

I think how can I be good for a family when I cannot even be True to myself?

CONSTRUCTIVE

&

DESTRUCTIVE THINKING

It is our light, not our darkness, that most frightens us.

Nelson Mandela

Today I arrive early and occupy the same seat we have sat at for the last two days. I have not spoken to mother in the last twenty-four hours nor have I been into the workplace. My line manager informed me I would need a doctors' note if I planned on being absent from work any longer, so I have scheduled an appointment with the doctor for this afternoon because I have no plans to return to the college until I have completed the lessons with Daryl.

I think about him and wonder where he has come from. He does not have a local accent and he said he was instructed to come and meet me by G.O.D. - the same being that will Call me. Does this then mean that is he in communication with Him on a daily basis? If I was to tell some people about my recent experience, about the conversations with Daryl and topics such as G.O.D., the Ego-Self, and Life Plans programmed into D.N.A. codes, they would think that I was crazy. I feel these are subjects that must be kept taboo, as though I am entering a restricted zone at my own risk.

It makes me wonder why there are only a very small percentage of people who do achieve great happiness in their life. For many years I assumed it was because they were lucky but I am starting to believe different. Did they risk everything and respond to the Call?

"A penny for your thoughts?"

"Oh, hello," I reply. "I was miles away."

"That's not such a bad thing," Daryl says as he sits down, "as long as you were using your mind for *Constructive* thinking and not *Destructive* thinking."

He sees the look on my face, and smiles.

"Destructive thinking?" I ask. "Is there such a thing?"

"Oh yes. And that is the topic of today's lesson. But, before we begin, I want you to tell me what you have learnt about yourself and if you understand the meaning of the Ego-Self and the True-Self."

I tell him the conclusions I have come to and how I arrived at them. He seems pleased when I tell him about the wild horse and how I saw myself leading people to spiritual freedom. He congratulates me on being a good student and, even though I blush, it feels good to know I am doing something right.

"So you see Jane the answers are inside of you. All it takes is a peek within."

When Daryl says this I imagine myself as a small child peeking into a dark space. I reach out and pull a light switch and there, inside the space, is a treasure trove filled with gold and jewels. It feels as though I am in Aladdin's cave and have just discovered a long kept secret, a place dripping with wealth and mystery, and it is mine to run around in and investigate at my own leisure

"Lesson number three: Constructive and Destructive Thinking."

I naturally reach for my bag and remove a notepad and pen, then write down the words he has just spoken.

Daril continues. "I want you to take a moment to think about these two words – Constructive and Destructive – and what they mean to you."

"Well," I reply after a short pause, "Destructive is something that does damage – to people, to property, to the environment. I think it means to have a negative effect: to destroy something."

"And Constructive?"

"That means to build something: to construct. It has a positive image to it. At the college I aim to give constructive feedback to students by speaking to them in terms of strengths and general areas for improvement, rather than highlighting apparent weaknesses. The goal is to be as kind as possible in order to help build a persons' confidence."

"You are correct in what you are saying. Constructive means building to serve or improve, and Destructive is as you say: the causing of or tending to cause destruction, which in itself is the act of destroying and bringing to ruin."

"So if thinking is either Constructive or Destructive, are you implying that people can actually bring themselves to ruin based solely on the way they think?" I ask, surprised.

"Correct. Surely you have heard statements like *You are what you think,* and *the mind maketh the man?*"

"Well, yes, but I thought they were clichés."

"Everything you see around you, all manmade things, started off in the mind. Every thought therefore is a cause and every condition an effect."

"But for that to be the case, it implies that I must take some sort of responsibility for the way I think!" I reply, surprised.

"That is correct Jane, and for this reason it is absolutely essential that you control your thoughts so as to bring about only desirable conditions."

"How am I meant to do that? My mind goes crazy at the best of times. It's like it's on constant overdrive and literally has a mind of its own, as though it is its own ruler irrespective of my wishes."

"You have to develop the art of controlled thinking. They key is to eliminate Destructive thoughts and nurture only Constructive thoughts."

He sees the look of surprise on my face. Nobody has ever spoken to me before about the power of the mind and the need to control its thoughts.

"Destructive thoughts will *initially* ruin only one person, and that is you. If you decide to enact these Destructive thoughts, then you will also bring to ruin those around you. Think of this moderate scenario: You are afraid of dogs because of an experience you had as a child. You carry that fear throughout your life. You have children, and every time you pass a dog you become frightened. What effect do you think this will have on your children?"

It doesn't take a genius to work this out. "The child will also have a fear of dogs, because he *thinks* that is how he should react to them."

"Yes, but the child has nothing to be fearful of. He is simply imitating what he sees from those around him." I nod in agreement.

"Now, let's take a look at something not so obvious. You have a fear of love and commitment, don't you?"

His question surprises me. What he is saying is true, but I have not told him this. I nod in agreement.

"Do you know why you fear these things? After all, love *is* the greatest emotion known to mankind and commitment *is* necessary to build values and trust within society."

I think for a moment and my mind flashes to mother. She always tells me 'don't trust anybody Jane because people are only after one thing and that is looking after themselves. You are a good catch for any man, because you have a good job and are intelligent, so don't be fooled by what they say. You can still have a family,' she reminds me, 'without the need for a man in your life. Stay independent. Men will only bring you down.'

Then I think about Francois, my ex-boyfriend. We spent the best part of four years together but the relationship was troubled after just several months into it. For a reason that only he will know, he decided to bed his ex-girlfriend and, although I tried, I never got over it. In the relationship I felt lonely and I could not trust him, even though I wanted to. After a few beers my insides would turn and my anger and frustration would unleash on him. Why I continued in such a destructive situation is beyond me, but I clung to this fragile relationship until it dissolved and there was nothing left to hold onto.

Physical scars can be seen: emotional and mental scars are hidden from view. After Francois and I separated, it was not until I was shown interest from other suitors that these unhealed wounds actually surfaced. Even though I had gotten rid of the source of my pain, I had failed to heal the intense damage done. Because of this, intimate relationships with other people were seriously flawed because I tended to focus on every minute weakness of theirs, causing me to become frustrated and filled with contempt for them. I craved companionship though wasn't prepared to give more of myself than was necessary. Many hours were spent feeling inadequate, questioning whether I could ever find true love.

One side of me believes in the existence of a love so great that it defies all logic: a love so strong that even nature yields in its presence. Where this exists, and who it exists for, I do not know. It is the side of me that believes in dreams, fairytales and the magic of life; the part of me who can relate to Cinderella and her deepest wishes coming true. The other side of me relates to the reality of life, where situations are meant to be harsh and nothing is perfect. This is what is prevalent in my surroundings: Headlines shouting about adulterous affairs; marriages breaking down because of betrayal; my father's insatiable desire for women outside the marital home.

"Yes," I reply to Daryl. "I do know why I fear these things but it is understandable. I have been hurt very deeply in the past."

"The past," he says. "Note you said *in-the-past*."

I understand what he is saying, but the past is a part of me. It is something I have to accept and it is not going to go away simply because I wish it away. I think he reads my mind again.

"When you experience something, it exists to

teach you a lesson. From it you develop skills and understanding that enable your Spirit to develop and progress through life. You should be aware of an experience in its given moment, take its teachings, and then move onto the next experience. The past only becomes a problem when we refuse to let it go and we allow it to attach itself to us until it becomes a hindrance, therefore affecting everything we do. It is such attachments that build the Ego-Self."

"I can appreciate what you're saying, but some things you just cannot get over! It is not as easy as that."

"What you are telling me stems from a Destructive thought. You are convinced in your mind that you *cannot* get over something, yet how you view a situation will determine what you take from it and how you then integrate it into your life. Every experience will add or detract from your True-Self. The simple fact to remember is this: Constructive thoughts will ensure positive outcomes; Destructive thoughts will always reap negative outcomes. Fear is a Destructive thought."

I think about what he has said, still unable to comprehend it.

"Let me put it this way, in a manner you may understand," he says. "Tell me, what is the smallest building block in life, that which makes up all matter?"

"The atom," I reply.

"And what makes up the atom?"

"Neutrons and electrons, and they are held together by energy. I think there is even pure energy at the centre of the neutrons and electrons."

"Yes, pure energy. In reality, everything you see is in fact bundles of energy, all spinning at extremely high rates."

I nod in agreement.

"We have solids, liquids and gases. Some you can see, others you cannot. Now let's think about sound waves. What are they?"

"They are waves of energy, carried through the atmosphere."

"And the atmosphere?"

"Gases and hence energy," I reply.

"What do you think is the substance of thought," he asks.

I look at him and see the twinkle in his eye.

"Energy," I reply hesitantly, realizing that I have been drawn to the conclusion.

"Yes, energy! How many times have you said to somebody, I lack energy?"

"Loads!"

"How do you feel when you have bags of energy?"

"Great, ready to take on the world, although I don't have bags of energy very often."

"When do you lack energy?"

"Usually if I am feeling down or if I am not in the mood for doing something. I seem to lack energy at work. I find the environment quite depressing."

"And so do you think that your thoughts can cause you to lack energy?"

"Er, yes, I suppose so."

I think of mother and the many times I have picked up the phone to speak to her, feeling very enthusiastic about things, but after I have finished speaking with her I have felt lethargic and down in my mood. I think of the many times I have stepped over the threshold at work, and my insides have found their way to the outside with dread gripping me like a strangler's hand. In intimate relationships I have felt good until a pretty girl has been in our company and then I have felt threatened, thinking that no man can resist any woman and that together they are deceiving me behind my back. All of these factors have had detrimental effects on my mood, my outlook and my self-esteem.

"If you are thinking positive thoughts, how do you feel?"

"Excited, as if I can achieve anything and that life is a lot of fun."

"And if you are thinking negative thoughts?"

"Trapped in a dreary, unfulfilling life," I reply.

"Ok, so I think we can conclude that thoughts have a direct influence on your energy and your mood, and when thoughts are Constructive, i.e. positive, they greatly enhance your energy, outlook and feeling about yourself and life."

I nod.

Daryl laughs. "There are many thoughts going around in your head that you are not always aware of, and if you are not aware of them then how do you know whether they are Constructive or Destructive, and more so, how they are affecting your mood?"

"I think I know what you're getting at. I must become more aware of every thought in order to understand whether it will have a positive effect or a negative effect on me."

Daryl nods.

"And then what?" I ask.

"And then you have to get to work. You must weed out all Destructive thoughts, just as a master gardener uproots unwanted plants in his garden."

"Surely that's impossible!"

"There is your first Destructive thought. So eliminate it. Words such as *impossible*, *can't*, and *if only* – these all have negative connotations that will prevent you from fulfilling your Life Plan."

"How does this relate to the Call?"

"When your Call comes you might naturally assume a negative mind set, talking yourself out of something which is potentially very positive and beneficial to your life and the life of others. Positive and Constructive thoughts are woven from images of courage, strength, determination, like when you daydream about Jean D'Arc. When the Call comes and you are in this constructive frame of mind, you will respond to it because fear, in its many forms, does not enter your mind."

"You make this all sound like something out of a movie. I have a hard time convincing myself this is real."

"There you go again.........a Destructive thought! You are telling yourself you need to *convince* yourself in order to believe something, and that it is *hard* to do this. Let me offer you a different option. Why don't you simply experiment and draw your own conclusions, then you won't have to convince yourself of anything. Replace every negative thought with its positive equivalent and see what happens."

What Daryl suggest sounds appealing. He is not offering quick fix solutions or miracle cures but is advising me to experiment for myself. This makes sense! After all, my years of studying chemistry and physics were geared towards defining an aim, a method, gathering results and drawing conclusions.

"Yes, I can do that." I reply. "But where do I start?"

***

Loud banging on the front door wakes me from my slumber. It is the middle of the night. I swing my legs over the side of the bed and, in a half sleep state, put on a dressing gown. As I walk down the stairs the banging gets louder and from the commotion outside the door it sounds like there is more than one person desperately trying to get into the house.

"Hang on," I yell, "I'm coming!"

"Open up," a voice shouts back, "or else we'll bash this door down!"

I turn the key and before I can turn the handle the door is forced open. It feels like I am caught in the middle of an elephant stampede as many people fight their way into the house. My shout of *stop, what are you doing!* is ignored, and people keep coming into the house, as if from out of nowhere. They flee in all directions: some upstairs, some into the downstairs rooms, and some out into the back yard. There must be nearly one hundred people in the house paying no regard for the fact that I am here and this is *my* property!

I enter the front room and see drawers being ransacked and electrical equipment being yanked from its socket. Women fall down the stairs, fighting over garments of clothing. Windows in the back room are being smashed for fun and still more people keep entering the house. A man and woman standing at the door ask me *is this a free party?*

Anger wells up in my stomach as I see the destruction that is being caused. I open my mouth to shout but nothing comes out except dead silence. I try again, this time filling my lungs and erupting forth with a verbal attack, but there is no sound: my mouth is void of all words.

Something strange is happening to my tongue. It is swelling inside my mouth, getting bigger and bigger and bigger. I feel it pushing against the sides of my throat and forcing my mouth open. In a state of panic I try to pull it with my hands. Chunks of tongue come away in my fingers and I feel blood trickling down my throat, causing me to cough and splutter. Then my tongue starts to curl up, lodging itself in my windpipe until I am choking. My eyes cry out *Please, help me*, but nobody notices: they are too busy invading my home.

I thrust my hand into my mouth and locate the tongue again, pulling as hard as I can to dislodge it. Using all my strength and will power I manage to yank it out, like a tree being uprooted by a violent wind storm. I stand at the doorway with the tongue in my blood soaked hand and a look of pained bewilderment on my face. I have no screams and my pleas make no sound, as though they have drowned in the thick, red, warm liquid which fills the cavity of my open mouth. *Somebody*, my insides call out, *please............ help me!*

My body is drenched in sweat and I feel cold. The clock reads 3.28 a.m. and I am alone. The street light outside casts its glow through the lace curtains and I hear cats calling out for mates in the silence of the night. This is the sixth night in a row that I have had a nightmare and it is getting to the stage where I am reluctant to go to sleep.

I get out of bed and run a hot bath, thinking about the nightmare and what it means. It is clear to me and I see it bears resemblance to what Daryl was saying earlier on. He had talked about thoughts and the importance of eliminating Destructive thoughts from my mind. He called the mind a personal palace, a Kingdom, and told me that I must know at all times *who* is entering this place. When a person has no control over the mind he said that it is like admitting everyone and anyone into your house, without any rules or guidelines to which they must conform. He asked me if I would hang a sign outside my home that read 'Everybody welcome, especially thieves, liars and beggars.' Of course I wouldn't I told him because you could never trust those people in your house. He said this was like the mind.

The Kingdom of the Mind is the place that is mine and mine alone. When thoughts are not controlled, I put the sign outside my house and any thought, irrespective of its intent, is welcome. These thoughts are the result of past thinking and every day interactions and activities, when thousands of impressions, ideas, prejudices and other forms of thought are imprinted upon my mind without me ever questioning their origin. Some effects are obvious, but most are subtle, and my only knowledge that certain thoughts have found somewhere to hang-out in my Kingdom is by experiencing the aftermath, which usually presents itself as traits within the personality:

the Ego-Self.

When I asked Daryl how I could control the thoughts that entered my Kingdom, he told me to imagine Buckingham Palace - the Queens residence. He asked me what would happen if there were no admittance controls to the Palace. This was obvious: it would be a free for all, with people coming and going as they please. There would be some people who meant good and others who wanted to inflict harm on Her Majesty, for example terrorists. To control this and eliminate the danger, there were strict admittance procedures with only known and authorized people being allowed to enter. Guards stand at all times on the gates, and top level security systems are in place around the perimeter of the Palace to ensure that people with dangerous intent cannot get near to the Queen and threaten her safety

Daryl said that this is how I am to view my mind. The people are the thoughts, wanting to get inside the Palace, but at present there are no admittance procedures in my mind: it is a free for all. To control the thoughts that enter I am to imagine a system which subjects each thought to careful analysis before it enters and, if the thought is of a Destructive nature, it is to be turned away.

"See Destructive thoughts like the people who want to inflict hurt and danger on the Queen," he said, "whose only intent is Destructive, not Constructive, participation. Your mind in its current state is run by these mental terrorists, and it must stop. Ask yourself: who is in control – you, or them?"

I step into the bath and feel hot water around my toes. I immerse the rest of my body in the tub and continue thinking about yesterdays' visit with Daryl. He caused me to question many things – about my life, my mental outlook, and my relationship with others. He said that what I see in the world is a reflection of what is inside of me. The frustration that I feel at others is really the frustration that I have with myself. He said that the common annoyances which cause me to react in some circumstances are nothing more than mirrors of my personality and the Ego-Self I have established. He showed me how the Ego-Self and the way I think are interlinked, and how the Spirit is ultimately forged by Will Power and that Will Power is a free gift from G.O.D. available for anyone to use if they decide to. Will Power is the inherent desire to choose to do something, a desire so strong that it can break habits in a single moment, changing even the Ego-Self if we choose to.

He said I could change my perception on love and commitment simply by changing the way I *think* about it. A reaction to any situation can be controlled and by substituting the negative thoughts I have at any given moment for positive, uplifting and inspiring thoughts, I will begin to function from a different level.

As if reading my thoughts he gave the example of jealousy, and stated it was a feeling that stems from insecurity in oneself. This insecurity is a feeling that one is not good enough or is in some way inferior to his fellow man. These are negative thinking habits because how can a man decide if he is better or worse than the person standing next to him based on shallow perception alone? Then he asked me, what makes a man or woman great? I was not too sure about the answer but I had some opinions. I believed a person who reached extreme happiness in their life symbolized greatness, because they were able to see and enjoy the beauty of life. This was the right answer. Happiness is worn by man and resembles the finest garments of clothing fashioned from the choicest of cloth, hand stitched by the greatest designer. Those who respond to the Call fulfill their Life Plan - their unique destiny - which guarantees happiness in this lifetime. Happiness makes a man look youthful and carefree, and it is a source of nourishment to his soul.

"A source of nourishment?" I asked.

"Yes. Uplifting thoughts bring with it wonderful health benefits because of the positive energy associated with them. Negative thoughts, such as jealousy and guilt, deprive the body of its health. The negative energy of these thoughts will affect vital organs and other systems within the body. People whose minds are out of control usually suffer illness - sometimes severe illness - at periods in their life."

My thoughts turn to mother. For years now it seems as though she has had ailments, from random aches and pains in the body, to teeth problems and diabetes which needs monitoring on a daily basis. Her attitude is that the world is a make or break situation and that only a few are lucky to make it. She was one of the unlucky ones. Mother blames *her* mother for many of her dilemmas, and feels an idiot for being fooled by the two men in her life: my father and my step father. 'If people aren't clever Jane, they are cunning. When people enter a relationship it is on the basis of what each can get out of it, not what they can put into it!' she says.

Controlling the mind has to start now: today! Anybody can decide to think differently at any given moment. It is never too late, nor too early. If a person is not happy in their life, then they must first look at the way they think.

Daryl told me a story about a young woman who was disappointed with the men she would get involved with. They felt justified in never being on time for a meeting or date, and in many cases would not call to say they were running late. The young woman started to avoid relationships because of the hassle and upset these situations brought her. It wasn't until she was advised one day to look at *herself* before judging another that she was able to change the cycle. Her analysis showed her that she was rarely punctual in her daily dealings and, because of this, she was sending a signal to others that it was OK to be late. When she finally committed to change herself and her own perception of time, others around her changed.

Daryl also told me a tale about the Shaolin monks. Apparently they can control their minds to an extent where they slow their heartbeat and can cause their body to enter into a state of hibernation. One of the tests of mind control is the drying of a wet sheet placed around the body. The monks are challenged to stand in below freezing temperatures, wearing nothing but the wet sheet, which they are to dry with their body heat. The monks focus their thoughts so intensely and precisely that they are able to raise their body temperature until they feel no cold at all, eventually drying the sheet.

This story amazes me. I asked him why more people don't know about the power of the mind. I have been through Sixth-Form College and University, studying with some intelligent people, and yet nobody ever told me about the mind and how it can be used for such feats. In all my time and interactions with people I have never known about how powerful the mind can be. Why is this?

He said that many people do not want to make the effort to understand the mind and use it for greatness. The majority reaches a mental comfort zone and would rather reside in that, with or without disappointment, then seek to actively change it. Because somebody is a qualified teacher does not guarantee they are disciplined and mentally controlled individuals. More often than not in society, intelligence is measured by exams, but there is nothing intelligent about a person who has a list of high flying qualifications and yet has no control over his mind, or no knowledge of to how to use it correctly. He reminded me that Jean D'Arc was illiterate – she couldn't read or write – but her accomplishments are a vital part of history and are seen as miraculous to many people. She used her mind for a definite purpose but she supported the power of her mind with Faith.

"Faith," he said, "because a man can achieve mighty feats if he is driven by Faith." This was the secret of Jean D'Arc's success.

FAITH

I am not afraid.....I was born to do this.

Jean D' Arc

I walk as fast as my legs will carry me. It is 11. 38 a.m. and I have arranged to meet Daryl by the Statue between 11 and 11.30. I recall him saying on the first day that he would wait only thirty minutes. My mind speaks, saying 'please, let him be there.' These meetings have become a necessity for me: a life line. Daryl has so much wisdom to pass on and I don't want to miss out on any of it. He is giving me just seven days of his time.

I start to berate myself, asking why I was so stupid to go back to sleep? My mind gets defensive and replies it is because I was tired. I argue that I should have slept in the night and have been more receptive to the alarm clock. A voice inside moans about the tone of the alarm and how it can't stand the sound of it, then all of a sudden I hear STOP! *This is not necessary.* I pause in my steps and take stock of my head, realizing I am battling with the terrorist within when I should be *choosing* how to think. This is what Daryl means when he says to take control of my thoughts.

The situation is really quite simple: I went back to bed, fell into a deep sleep, and did not allow enough time to prepare for the meeting. No blame, no arguments. It is *my* responsibility: my error. There is a lesson in this which I must learn. A mistake is only negative if the lesson is not learned.

I turn the corner and see the Statue. The benches surrounding it are empty, devoid of any life. People hurry in and out of shops but I do not see Daryl. My heart sinks and I feel disappointed. The mind proceeds to beat me up and to tell me that I am an idiot, but I tell it to *STOP! You are not to think until I say so.* It feels as though I am training a wild dog, a beast that has no conception of control. Train it fairly, with discipline, and it will become your best friend. Show too much aggression, and it may spend its days in fear of you, waiting for its chance to attack.

The Statue wears the same expression: it never changes. Rain falls onto the top of her head and she looks like she might be trying to pull the shawl tighter around her shoulders. Her calf looks content, un–phased by the damp weather. Nobody sits next to her today. It is one of those grey overcast Northern days – damp, dark and determining the mood of many people.

My heart feels like it is sinking, as though I may have forfeited a great opportunity for learning because I was foolish enough to go back to bed, but something inside of me says don't worry. It is not a problem. It is how it is.

I walk over to the Statue knowing that she is always here for me, come rain or shine. Then I notice that today she clasps something more in her hands. Stuffed tightly in her firm grip is a transparent bag containing a small white envelope. I ease the bag free and see that my name, Jane, is written on the front of the envelope in Daryl's now familiar handwriting. My heart starts to beat fast, excited at the prospect of what is inside. Not wanting to get the envelope wet in the rain, I put it in my pocket and head for the nearest café. As I walk, large colourful posters in the travel agent's window catch my eye. I am drawn to the golden beaches and clear blue sea. It looks lovely: an obvious paradise. A yearning fills my chest, a yearning to walk in and book a holiday. Their advertising campaign has nearly worked, the only downfall being I can't afford a holiday at the present time.

The reason I can't afford a holiday is because I spend a lot of money on socializing and buying alcohol. It has been my main way of escape to date. I have thought many times about changing my habits but something stops me. Perhaps it is the thought of not knowing what else to do. If I could choose I would jump on a plane this very moment - embarking on an adventure and writing about it as it unfolds. But these things aren't done. Or are they? Is this a Destructive thinking habit that Daryl has spoken about? Writing off situations because people around me do not do them? And I realize I have just used the words *if I could choose*? Surely, if I cannot choose what to do with my life, then who can?

Then it hits me. *I am* choosing. What I am doing with my life now *is* choosing. I am choosing to work a job I do not receive fulfillment from; I am choosing to cling on to past situations, continuing to allow them to affect me in the present day; and I am choosing to live out contrived roles that other people expect of me without ever truly expressing what is in my heart.

A massive unseen weight lifts from my shoulders, and I feel like I am waking up from a lifetime spent in state of amnesia.

***

Sheltered from the rain inside the cafe, I slowly unfold the contents of the envelope. On a single piece of A4 paper, in Daryl's neat handwriting, is a note. It reads:

Dear Jane, I trust you are comfortable and ready to start today's lesson. It is another simple insight which will aid you on your journey and serve the purpose of allowing you to respond to the Call.

Many years ago I met a blind lady, Helen. She had been blind since childhood. Her father died when she was an infant and her mother raised her single handedly. It was at a time when financial assistance from the Government was not common, hence many of Helens early years were spent in poverty. Her mother knew that one day she would die and leave her blind daughter alone to fend for herself in what she saw as a cruel world. Because of this, she forced Helen to be independent. She encouraged her to listen to sounds, to feel her way around an environment based on the way sounds are reflected. Over and over again she told her "Helen, do not become a cripple. Your other senses must become your eyes. Have Faith in them, and see!"

When Helen was nineteen years of age her mother died, and she felt an overwhelming sense of loneliness. Even though she was in the midst of friends there was a deep feeling of emptiness and isolation. This feeling inspired a spirit of unrest that drove her on and on in fruitless search upon the outside for what she later learned could only be obtained from within. This discovery prepared her for the Call of G.O.D.

When I met Helen, I did not know she was blind. She moved and acted like a person with full sight. In her short lifetime she has become one of the world's most renowned business women. She is a multi-millionaire and does extensive work for charity. Her mission, she believes, is to give sight to the blind, irrespective of how functional a persons' eye's are.

And how does she do this? By the simple belief system of

Walk by Faith, and not by sight, because Faith is the root of all senses.

And this is the topic of today's lesson.

Because you missed our meeting, I am unable to assist you further, so I suggest that you use your time wisely. Find out as much as you can about Faith and how it applies to your life.

I will be at the Statue between 11 and 11. 30 tomorrow morning. We have two lessons left and then I move on.

I sincerely hope you will be there. The best is yet to come!

> *Yours, in friendship*
> *Daryl*

One side of me kicks myself because he is not sat here explaining in more detail the subject of Faith. The other side is telling me that I have the resources and ability to learn about Faith myself, but I must *desire* to do so and then use what is at hand.

I drink my coffee and leave the café. On the other side of the street I see Shelly, a friend I sometimes socialise with. She calls out to me and starts walking in my direction. After general greetings she says,

"Hey Jane, have you heard about Mick?"

"Heard what?"I reply.

"He's dead."

I feel a blow to my chest.

"When did this happen? I was talking to him on Monday afternoon."

"Monday night. Apparently he OD'd."

"OD'd?"

"Yes. He had been experimenting with a drug called the Simeon Effect. He decided to take a double dose and never came out of it. His parents found him on Tuesday morning. From what I have heard the police are trying to trace whoever sold him the drug."

"Really!"

"Yeah. I'm surprised you have not seen the newspapers."

"No. I have been in my own world lately."

"Why? What have you been up to?"

"Er, meeting with a stranger and talking about life!"

"Mm, sounds interesting. Is he sexy?"

I can see the expectancy in Shelly's eyes. She always is one for gossip, keeping herself up-to-date on the goings on in other peoples' lives. She is known for asking the obvious questions that other people want to ask but don't in the name of politeness.

"Look, I've got to go. I have some research to do," I reply.

"No need to be a dark horse Jane. You're secret is safe with me," she says, giggling.

"Well, I am actually going to the library to learn about Faith," I reply.

"Now *that's* funny," she says, clearly thinking I am joking with her. "As far as I'm concerned you need Faith in one thing and one thing only……. and that's your mirror. It never lies. If you look rough, it tells you. If you look good, it tells you!"

We both laugh and I make my excuses and leave.

The dictionary defines Faith as: *the assured expectation of things hoped for, the evident demonstration of realities though not yet beheld. A strong or unshakeable belief in something.*

I think for a moment, questioning how this relates to what Daryl has taught me already. He introduced the concept of G.O.D. at our first meeting, telling me that G.O.D. is the Giver of Destiny and that He has programmed me with a unique Life Plan which is locked in the code of my D.N.A. To unlock the code and hence fulfill my destiny, I must heed the Call of G.O.D. and I can only do this by speaking His language. To heed the Call results in true happiness in life.

At a given point in my life G.O.D. will *call* on me to make a choice, one which will affect the outcome of my life. By ignoring the Call, I tell G.O.D. that I do not want to claim the destiny that He, or It, has set for me. Therefore, He will go away and let me be until I decide to reach out for Him.

This Call can come in several ways, but only by having a controlled mind will I recognize it when it comes. To have a controlled mind means to be aware of every thought which enters it, paying close attention to Destructive and Constructive thoughts. A Destructive thought will bring ruin in one way or another, whereas a Constructive thought will energise and uplift me. Both types of thought will affect those around me.

Everything is made up of energy, and it is a known fact that energy can neither be created nor destroyed: it is simply converted from one form to another. Like attracts like, and so negative will find negative, and positive, positive. The conditions with which I meet in the world without correspond to the conditions I find in the world within, and these conditions are based on the way I think. Everything I think has an effect, and good actions will spring from a mind disciplined in Constructive thoughts, not

Destructive thoughts.

When I choose to accept my destiny, I will have learned to speak the language of G.O.D. and my actions will reap rewards for many people. Daryl has now introduced the element of Faith, the next building block. From the definition I realise that I am to trust and believe in G.O.D. and what He has planned for me. This sounds easy, but is it? Does this mean that I am to give myself wholly to Him and submit myself to whatever fate He decides? If this is the case, what if I am required to do things that are not quite what I want? I hear Daryl's voice. He says, 'Remember the Ego-Self and the True-Self.'

My reasoning is acting from the Ego-Self, the aspect of my personality based on my limited perception of things and past ways of thinking, irrespective of whether it makes me happy. This reasoning is fear based and therefore looks for excuses to *turn away* from an opportunity rather than to *embrace* it. The True-Self is connected to G.O.D. and therefore does not reason in this way for it knows that my unique Life Plan will bring me happiness and contentment. Instead of doubtful questioning, the True-Self applies insight to ensure that my thought and attention is turned in the right direction. Daryl said that insight is a kind of human telescope and it enables me to examine facts and conditions at long range.

I think of Helen's statement: walk by Faith, not by sight. If I walk by sight then I am living my life based on what I see around me in my day to day dealings: follow the fashions, climb the career ladder, settle down and get married with two point four children. If I walk by Faith, I am allowing my True-Self to be guided by G.O.D, listening to His directions through my senses – sight, sound, touch, taste and feel. I am not concerned about what people are wearing or what car they are driving, I am concerned only with connecting to the heartbeat of life and developing my own personal rhythm.

The dictionary states that Faith is a strong or unshakeable belief in something; an assured expectation of things hoped for. Therefore, for my hopes to become a reality I must have the Faith that they are *already* a reality, but how can I go from not having Faith to having Faith? Or, do I already have Faith but Faith in my fears and not in my hopes, like my mother?

I find myself wishing Daryl was here to answer

my questions, but he is not, so I have to look at other options. In the library I am surrounded by books on every subject and I have access to the internet. 'You must first seek to know and then the answer will reveal itself,' I hear him saying. I wonder where Daryl got his knowledge from. He seems to be a vast source of wisdom. Then I remember the book, Universal Intelligence, which he always carries with him. This will be my starting point.

An internet source tells me that Universal Intelligence was written over 5000 years ago, and is a charting of the history of mankind. Contained within the book are the most fundamental laws of life, laws which enable man to work in harmony with G.O.D. It explores these laws through fables, proverbs and real life stories, and also has information about the consequences incurred when man chooses to ignore the ways of G.O.D.

I discover the work is in the public domain so I locate a website which has the full book and a search criterion. I type in How to Have Faith. The following passage is presented to me:

A man can acquire Faith at any moment in his life; a desire to know Faith will deliver Faith. To know Faith, man must enter into active prayer with G.O.D. Prayer can be undertaken in many forms and it is an individual decision as to how this is executed. Prayer is a time for contemplation and reflection, discussion and gratitude. When one enters into Prayer, he must trust that he is in direct communication with G.O.D. and therefore all words are heard. To doubt is to not have Faith. Faith will move mountains and cause miracles to occur. It is the most powerful force available to mankind.

I think about the word *prayer*. It holds strange feelings for me because in my life I only ever prayed when I was a child. In the school assembly I would chant, like a robot, the Lord's Prayer, and at night before I slept I would pray that my family were kept safe. In times of sadness I have prayed, although afterwards felt somewhat silly for believing that there was something out there looking down on me and hearing what I was saying.

But how does this relate to what Daryl was telling me about energy? Everything is made up of energy, which has been proved scientifically. During my degree course, I learned that electrons which form atoms fill all space and exist everywhere; that they are omnipresent. I also know that everything has a source, from rivers and streams, to electrical systems. It is a common term when talking about errors and problems to refer to the *source* of that problem. So energy too will have a source.

Nature is a constant exchange of energy: it gives and takes back. Everything that lives has periods of birth, growth, fruitage and decline, from people to plants. Seas change direction; the winds blow throughout the world; the seasons change and the animals in nature react to these seasons. Everything works in perfect harmony with everything else, and it all connects back to the one omnipresent source, a source which directs the whole of life. From what I have learnt with Daryl, this great source is G.O.D. the Creator and Master Programmer of all of these things, and it is It, or Him, whom I connect with when praying.

But what benefits will it bring? I understand I have been led to the notion of Prayer in my search for Faith, and because G.O.D. has programmed me and knows how I am to fulfill my Life Plan, that Prayer is *our* time, a sort of private conversation between us. He will respond to my questions and show me the direction to take so that everything I do is in harmony with His ways and the plans He has for me. This makes life so easy, because it means I will not have to toil or worry myself with anything because He is working it all out for me. All I must do is act and rely upon His never failing response to bring about everything I need to fulfill my Life Plan, a Life Plan chosen by Him. In reality then it is *His* work, and not mine, that I am doing.

I am beginning to understand why my life is currently not how it can ultimately be. This frustration I feel is because *I* allow my life to be guided by people, by those around me, who have many opinions on many subjects. I have spent most of my years being influenced by my mother, teachers, colleagues and friends, and I have unconsciously allowed them to be the authority on how I should live *my* life because I have not known how to fully immerse myself in the glory of life.

A dog knows no different either. It is trained in how to obey. Yes, it will always have its animal qualities, but if it is taught to beg for food, it will do. If it is trained to stop at the side of the road, it will do so. And this is what I have become: an obedient dog.

But now I am being offered something much greater. I am being offered an adventure, a journey, an experience which is *my* life and mine alone.

Prayer is such a fundamental part of Faith because it keeps me breathing the untainted air of life, connecting me with G.O.D. - the one source of energy. It is Faith in this source which will cause me to fulfill my destiny.

I search for articles relating to Jean D'Arc. Her actions were pure, innocent and devoid of selfishness. Guided by Her Faith in G.O.D. Jean defied all learned logic in her quest to defeat the English and crown the rightful heir to the throne of France. She was loyal and dedicated to her cause because she knew her destiny was given from G.O.D. and she held His ways in reverence. Mighty feats were achieved by Jean because she gave her Spirit over to her Creator, not fearing the bloody, brutal battles she was to encounter, but trusting with all her heart the Call of G.O.D. and his chosen mission for her.

So where do I start? I suppose it is quite simple: I will have Faith that G.O.D. will reveal His plan for me; that he will unveil my unique destiny. I will have Faith that what I am learning is the key to a greater life, and will trust that, at all times, I am being cared for and nurtured by the one source of energy that created me.

And how will I pray? I will use my love of writing as my chosen method of Prayer because it is during this time that I am the most free with my expression.

By using my imagination and my pen I will enter into the silence and connect with G.O.D.

IMAGINATION

Logic will get you from A to B. Imagination will take you everywhere.

Einstein

"Imagination – the key to the treasure trove locked within, and the topic of today's lesson."

It feels exciting sitting next to Daryl. I am eager to tell him all I had learned yesterday in his absence and how, last night and this morning, I had prayed by writing down my thoughts and opening my heart to G.O.D. At first the praying felt strange, but my feelings soon dissipated when I reminded myself of the reason for praying. My nightmares did not happen last night and today I feel on fire: raring to go. I cannot remember the last time I felt so good, so alive, and so full of energy.   Mother has left several messages on the answer machine asking me to contact her but I have not felt the need. Normally I feel guilty if I don't speak with her at least once every two days, but I do not have this feeling today. I don't even feel selfish for taking this time for me because I have Faith that it is all a necessary part of my progress and that the outcome of what I am doing will have a greater impact on my life than not phoning mother for a few days.

"The Imagination can be mans greatest friend or his worst enemy and is linked to the way a person thinks, as we discussed in Lesson Three. Many times we fail to use our Imagination to its full potential and, because we develop such bad habits of under use, it begins to atrophy......."

"What do you mean, atrophy?" I interrupt.

"It will start to decay and cease to function normally. An unused Imagination is like a voice that is never heard. Imagination is the key to all great achievements and what seem, to the naked eye, like impossible feats. It basically allows you to see without eyes, just like Helen."

I think about the last time I used my Imagination. As a child I would write fictitious stories set in fantasy lands, or picture myself traveling the world. More recently I imagined myself leaving work for good and then just packing a bag and going to a foreign destination – like the one on the poster at the travel agents.

"You use your Imagination far more than you realise Jane. Each time you envisage a conversation between yourself and another person, you are using your Imagination. Every time you think about events in your mind, maybe acting out scenarios and what-if situations, you are using your Imagination. The essence here though is in using your Imagination to create the life you want and using it only for positive purposes.

You can even use your Imagination to counteract the effects of negative situations that have occurred in your life."

"What, I can repair the damage that a negative situation has caused?"

"Yes. The repair will be to your Ego-Self and hence will allow you to let go of the traits you have developed as a form of self protection: traits which hinder your progress in life. These traits are the ones which prevent you from revealing your True-Self."

I think again about Francois. Whenever he comes to mind my stomach does cartwheels. Feelings surface which make me feel as though I could punch him in the head, shout at him, grab hold of him and shake him. I think how foolish he was to betray me and lose my trust in him. I sense Daryl is reading my mind.

"Close your eyes and imagine yourself standing in a place that is calm and peaceful," he instructs.

I do as Daryl says and, after a few minutes, I see myself standing in a clearing in a wood. The sun's rays penetrate the gaps between the leaves of trees, bathing my body in warmth. I hear birds singing the joys of summer, and feel the cool grass underneath my bare feet.

"Absorb your surroundings through your senses, and allow the atmosphere to seep into your skin. Feel your body waking up, becoming light and child like. How do you feel?"

My eyes still closed, I tell Daryl I feel relaxed and happy. The image is strong in my mind and I feel as though I am actually in the place that I am imagining.

"There is somebody standing nearby who has hurt you deeply at some point in your life. Welcome that person into your presence and embrace them, tell them that you understand and forgive them for the hurt they have caused you."

My heart starts to beat faster so I tell myself to relax. The person who is standing underneath a tree is Francois. He has a look of sadness in his eyes. I see myself holding my arms out to him and motioning for him to come closer. For the first time since our relationship ended I feel in control and have a sense of pity for him.

As he walks towards me I see that he, too, is vulnerable and confused. He is not as confident as what he portrays in real life and is, in reality, no different to me: someone trying to make sense of the world and find their place in it. When he reaches me I hold his hands and imagine myself telling him that everything is OK now. 'I forgive you Francois', I say to him, 'and I understand why you acted in the way you did. We are not bound by our emotions, only by our mind. Our emotions are a reflection of how we perceive things. If you knew you would have caused me such great hurt, you would not have acted in the way you did. But it is OK. I forgive you.' Francois smiles and I see a look of relief on his face.

My heart feels as though it is shedding weight, becoming lighter until it is virtually weightless in my chest. I tell him that I have to go now, and I thank him for coming into my life. 'We have shared a moment of time that will only be precious if we allow it to be,' I say to him. 'It is usually the greatest adversity which gives us the most strength, so let us remember the wonderful journey we both embarked on, and allow this memory to shine by taking the very best lessons that were given to us.'

As I speak to him I am amazed at the level of insight which comes from my mouth. It is as though I have tapped into a source of knowledge that surpasses anything I have experienced before. I am confident this is G.O.D, the source of life that Daryl told me about.

This place I have entered in my Imagination feels very real and I could stay here all day. Feelings I harboured against Francois are melting away and I find myself realizing they are of no relevance anymore. Only the lessons beneath the feelings will be of any benefit to me from now on and it is these lessons I must understand. Thinking about Francois in negative ways will serve no benefit to me, nor him, or anybody else. Only positive thoughts can lead to positive actions and imagining Francois in this way will enable me to think of him only in positive ways.

I sit on the grass and take a deep breath, closing my eyes and focusing on the sounds and smells which surround me.

"Slowly open your eyes Jane and bring yourself back to your actual environment."

Like a mole fresh out of hibernation, I return to Daryl's presence wide eyed and somewhat in awe at what I have just experienced. It is as though a change has taken place in me and I feel calm: at peace.

"You can call on the power of your Imagination at any time. Use it to heal wounds, to build emotional bridges, to channel your thoughts and to eliminate the fears that lurk in your soul. With your Imagination you can restore your health, build empires, effect great works for mankind. There are infinite possibilities. Your Imagination knows no bounds: everything is possible. You use your Imagination every day Jane, but you use it for detrimental purposes. Fears, worries, stress – they are all magnified by wrongly using the Imagination. Negative feelings, thoughts, habits etc are also deepened by the incorrect use of the Imagination. By possessing such a remarkable tool, you must know how to use it, and use it only for the highest good of mankind. The highest good is always established from positive means and therefore it is your responsibility to utilize your Imagination to ensure positive action. Anything less than this will lead to destruction: you will tamper with your destiny and bring ill effects into your life. Do you understand?"

"I am learning to understand," I reply.

"What you have just done is called a *visualisation*, where you use your senses to create a scene in your Imagination. I am going to set you a series of visualisations that I want you to complete before our next meeting: simple exercises in using the

Imagination. We will meet again tomorrow at the café. This will be our penultimate lesson, so any questions you have, then please bring them with you."

I thank Daryl for his time. As he stands I get the feeling that I want to hug him, to thank him for freely giving me his time. Since we met five days ago, I know there have been some major changes in my outlook. I am beginning to feel like a new person, as though I am going through a transformation which is changing my entire life.

"Do not prevent good thoughts and genuine feelings from flowing," he says with a smile on his face. I stand and hold out my arms to him.

"Thank you Daryl. Thank you very much."

***

The first task he set was for me to think about a situation which gave me cause for concern, and to use my Imagination to *heal* the situation. The key, Daryl said, was to hold the situation in my mind until it felt real, and then to send positive energy to it. The positive energy could be in a form which most distinguished its visual means, for example, a rainbow, a stream of bright white light, even a large red love heart, or anything else which signified positive energy to me. Stick with the familiar, he instructed, but use it in new ways.

As I lie on the bed, I bring an image of my work colleagues to mind. I see them sat in the staff room, talking amongst themselves. I walk into the room and they stop talking. I have a large grin on my face and I carry a handbag. 'What is in the bag?' I am asked.' A present for you,' I reply.

I reach into the bag and take out a small sphere of light. 'Hold out the palms of your hand,' I say, and in turn I place a sphere of light into each person's hands. As they look at the light their faces glow. 'This is a bundle of positive energy, for each of you. Place it over your heart and allow its goodness to seep into your body.'

They do as they are instructed and I see their bodies glow from the light that has entered them. Each one looks radiant, as though they have become young again. A white light surrounds each person and a feeling of calm fills the room.

For the second task I was instructed to think of a person who has control over me, someone whose words and moods affect my emotions. I think of mother. Using my Imagination, I am to devise a scene which would see me breaking the chains of control.

I hold myself in my mind's eye and I imagine I am stood with a large chain wrapped around my body. On the end of the chain is mother. First, I hand her a large red heart filled with love and respect. 'This is for you,' I say as I give it to her. 'I want you to understand that I will always love you, but I need more freedom from your ways. I understand that you love me, and that you only want the best for me, but the time has come for me to learn about life by enjoying my own experiences. To do that, I must cut these chains which tie us together. We will always have a special bond, but this bond does not need to feel restrictive.'

I take the chain in my hands and try to break it apart. Mother's response surprises me. 'You do not need to struggle like that love,' she says, 'you can simply unwind yourself from it.' She pulls the chain and I start to turn around on the spot, the chain becoming loose around my body. After several turns, the chain falls free. 'You could have done that at any time,' she says, 'but you chose not to.' Mother walks towards me and we embrace. We both hold the large red heart, and I see myself smiling.

The third and final task was more challenging, but Daryl said that visualization would become so easy that I could imagine myself anywhere, at anytime. Like anything, it takes practice, until it becomes a habit, but he was not going to elaborate on the topic of habits because that was the sixth lesson. Practice, practice and practice, he said.

In this task I am to think of an element of my personality which is hidden within, a side which never comes out in public but is always waiting patiently on the horizon of my thoughts. I imagine myself picking up my passport and setting off on a journey. I see myself passing through airport controls with a huge smile on my face, and I board a plane. Next I am sat on a sun lounger on a beach: white golden sands, turquoise waters. In front of me is a writing pad, and I am documenting my travel experience. There are no worries about where I must go, or who I need to see, because I am taking each moment as it comes, allowing the journey and hence story to unfold each day.

In the next scene, I am sat in a restaurant with a group of friends who are laughing and enjoying each other's company. My hair is long and my complexion healthy. A stranger walks up to me with a book in his hand. It is a book I have written and he asks me for an autograph.

I see myself being interviewed on TV about this book. It has become an international best seller and has changed people's lives. The interviewer asks 'Why do you think this book has become such a phenomenal success?' and I reply 'Because it encourages people to live their dreams and to fulfill their destiny, a form of encouragement that we all need, whatever language we speak or wherever we are located in the world.'

***

The alarm clock calls out to me long after I have already woken up. It has been a full night of unbroken sleep and I feel great. The sun is shining, birds are chanting their welcomes to the new day and the air smells fresh. I look in the mirror and see a spark in my eyes and I know that life is actually returning to my once limp body. I think about Mick, and how limp he is now: six feet under without ever fulfilling his destiny, his life wiped out in one foul swoop.

When I think of it, there is a lot of tragedy in the world: wars, murders, robberies. It is an endless list and one which could seem to dominate life if I choose to perceive it that way. What must be remembered is that there is much goodness and joy in life, but these aspects need a trained eye to fully appreciate their existence and beauty. It is easy to only focus on the negative aspects because these surround me on a daily basis. Horror stories and tragedies are what make newspapers sell, and therefore such stories dominate headlines, a vicious cycle that I do not need to buy in to.

Daryl taught me about controlling every thought which enters my mind and I have realised that to do this I must be very selective with the information that I feed it. There is no point in trying to eliminate negative thoughts when I spend my days reading gossip columns and tabloid newspapers. It is essential to also choose wisely the company I keep: anybody who causes me to feel inadequate because of their words, then I must limit the time I spend in their company. It is this last point that has caused me to think in more depth about the work role I have assigned myself to.

For the past year (at least) I have felt immense frustration at the attitude of colleagues and students. A day at the college leaves me feeling mentally and emotionally exhausted. There is a doom and gloom ethos prevalent in the department, one which seeks to find quick fix solutions to pass rates and statistics. Several staff make it quite clear they are only *hanging on* until retirement and that they have no interest in the job. Many hours are spent amongst colleagues and their continuous complaining about how things have changed for the worse and that they are not how they used to be. There is a very pessimistic outlook in the department and it is amongst this that I have positioned myself.

Students are not much different. There are handfuls that have aspirations, but the majority wants a qualification for the sake of having it, without expending much effort. Because everyone seeks an easy life, standards fall and enthusiasm dampens. It is a dog-eat-dog situation: a downward spiral into non-doing.

Because of this frustration and my inability to fit in, I have felt lost, as though something is wrong with *me*. Slowly my confidence has ebbed away and I have felt unsure of what I am doing and where my life is carrying me. I will admit that I have felt suicidal, and I have also felt murderous, as though I could annihilate a group of people just for the sake of it. This is why I relate to the Statue in the Square: an onlooker with a solid exterior, hard as stone, not wanting to move in case everything shatters; isolated and trapped in a body of resistance.

But I have been given a light, a torch that I can pick up and carry with me, to shine on my life and bring the dark areas of it into the open. There is nothing to be ashamed of because I see that I have been uneducated in the ways of the Mind and Spirit. Nobody has ever taught me about Life Plans, Ego-Self, Faith and Prayer, and the other topics Daryl has shared with me in these past few days. It feels as though I have learned more about life and how to live it in this last week than I have in my whole lifetime. It causes me to think about the validity of formal schooling and what it really does for a person. In conclusion I can say it makes man an average man, with the potential to be a good man, but it does not make a great man. A great man has to give himself to G.O.D. – the Giver of Destiny. Only by fulfilling one's unique Life Plan can he fully reveal the marvel of himself, because this has been chosen for this very reason. Anyone can achieve greatness if he decides to stop looking for quick fix solutions to his life, but the majority of mankind are cowards, hence why only a few achieve what appear like miraculous feats.

Today, with Daryl, is lesson number six. A tinge of sadness stabs at my heart because tomorrow is our last day together. Even now I do not know where he has come from or where he is going, but this is irrelevant in the scheme of what we are doing. At our second meeting I asked him these details and he said, 'Jane, where man has been and where man is going is small in comparison to what he is doing now. You are a culmination of everything that has been, and the decisions you make now will determine what you will do in the future. Your only duty in life is to live in the Spirit and follow the unique destiny as stored in your D.N.A. code, because only then is your happiness assured.'

I take out my notebook and look back at the lessons Daryl has taught me so far. There have been five lessons. Lesson number one was Life Plan and the importance of being ready for the Call, I imagine like hearing my very own lottery numbers being called out. Being ready for the Call means to hear it and distinguish it from the multitude of thoughts that swirl around in the mind, but to be able to do this I must learn the language of G.O.D.

The second lesson was about knowing myself in terms of Ego-Self and True-Self. There is a marked difference in that the Ego-Self is formed out of expected actions, fears and interests sparked by past circumstances: this is the personality. The True-Self acts from the Spirit, unscarred by anything that has occurred in life but aware and alert to the *lessons* of life. It is the Spirit that I must live from in order to know and fulfill my destiny. The personality driven Ego-Self will hamper my progress because it acts in irrational ways without reason and understanding.

To fully know the Spirit, that which resides within, I must become aware of my thoughts and the effect they have on me. There are two types of thought: Destructive and Constructive. This is lesson number three.

Spirit, the True-Self, will not terrorise itself with thoughts that may bring it to ruin, and negative, Destructive thoughts will do this. The personality feeds off such ways of thinking. Only positive, Constructive thoughts can serve the desired purpose necessary for fulfilling my destiny because the way I think will determine my perspective on life. To date I have been consumed with detrimental ways of thinking, but I can change this now by choosing to *think* differently. For every negative thought there is a positive equivalent, and by monitoring each thought that enters my mind I am in a position to select the positive option.

The fourth lesson on Faith was the most difficult because I was not in the presence of Daryl to answer my questions. Still, with effort, I learned and I understood. Faith is an unquestioning belief in G.O.D.'s plans. To have Faith is to know that G.O.D. is directing me and guiding me every step of the way. Faith must be backed by Prayer because it keeps me connected to this one great source of energy. Daryl told that me that few people know how to pray. They understand that there are laws governing electricity, mathematics and chemistry, but for some reason it never seems to occur to people that there are also spiritual laws that are definite, scientific, and exact, and they operate with precision. A triangle has three sides and its angles always add up to one hundred and eighty degrees. It does not matter how the triangle is drawn, how the angles vary, because this law will never change. A triangle will *always* have three sides and will *always* add up to one hundred and eighty degrees. Spiritual laws are the same. They cannot be altered, and therefore Prayer will *never* fail to yield results. Prayer backed by Faith, that is. This is one of G.O.D.'s guarantees.

Yesterday was lesson number five and the topic of Imagination, and I learned that this is a practical tool for healing and converting past situations as well as affecting future ones. Using the Imagination in negative ways can only lead to destruction, and using it in Constructive ways will only lead to positive actions and outcomes. A good tree cannot produce bad fruit, and a bad tree cannot produce good fruit. It is one of Life's basic laws.

HABIT

It's no good saying one thing and doing another.

Catherine Cookson

"You are making good progress Jane and I don't think I need to remind you that tomorrow will be our last meeting."

I look down at my feet, unsure of what to say. It is a moment I have been looking forward to and yet dreading at the same time. Looking forward to because Daryl will have revealed his seven secrets to me; dreading it because I will be left to my own devices.

"That is why our topic for today is Habit and the way we allow Habits to shape our lives and our experience."

The Statue still refuses to look at me. We sit in her view but her head remains turned towards the ground, unable to make eye contact with people around her. Was she too hoping that something would not come to an end; hoping that if she refused to look something or someone in the eye that time might stand still? Then again, time waits for nobody. It is the most valuable asset given freely to man, yet it is one which he so readily wastes. The rich, the poor, the child, the adult, the genius, the fool – we all have twenty-four hours in a day. Not one person can buy more, steal, sell, or add one single cubit of time to his life. We have an allotted amount, and all we have to do is *invest* it, wisely. Those whom invest their time view it as a priceless commodity which, if utilized to its maximum effect, will return great dividends.

Daryl continues. "You are right to think about time, because Habits can be one of the gluttonous creatures that devour it."

I change the subject and ask him, "How do you always know what I am thinking?"

He smiles, the sun causing him to squint as he looks at me. "Because it is written all over your face! When you learn to understand the mind, you can have a dialogue with the person who stands before you without them even knowing. Think back to lesson three, when I told you about people walking into your mind without your consent. Until you make Constructive thinking a Habit, your mind will have fatal weaknesses. But, it is not just the Habit of Constructive thinking: it is a combination of good, life enhancing Habits."

"Life enhancing Habits?".

"Yes. There are habits that revolve around your desires and you have habits that revolve around your fears. The Habits that revolve around your desires for health, happiness, financial independence, and success

136

are life-enhancing. On the other hand, the Habits which revolve around your fears act as brakes on your potential. They hold you back and interfere with your Life Plan."

I think about what Daryl has just said and know that he is right. There are occasions when I do something and I hear an inner voice say I should not have done that. In the workplace I find myself falling into the use of foul language and gossip, but afterwards when I walk away I feel annoyed with myself for having allowed it to happen. When I wake with a hangover and realize I have spent a considerable amount of money on alcohol, I feel disappointed with myself because it was not necessary, and I then spend the day feeling guilty over my actions.

"The only constant in life Jane is change. People are afraid of change and so they try to avoid it at all costs. It is easier to live with the detrimental, fear based Habits that we possess then it is to try and change them. Man likes the familiar: it is his safety zone. He prefers to stand on the sidelines and watch others put the effort in, and then if it doesn't work out he can yell I told you so. If it does work out, the same man will envy the progress of the individual who embraced change."

"Do you think that work is a fear based Habit?"

"If it is not in line with your destiny, or if you believe you need to move on but can't, then yes, it has become a detrimental Habit. It has become a comfort zone where you no longer challenge yourself and apply yourself fully. This is an area where most people fall into Habits, and the knock on effect is that they stop progressing as people, allowing the work environment to shape and mould them. They become like puppets, no longer in control of their life but carried along by convention and convenience."

He is hitting the nail on the head. Colleagues at work have openly admitted that they are on an easy number and besides they are too old to move onto another job now. They are used to how things are in the department: they know each other and they understand how things work.

"You must have courage Jane. You must embrace the change and not be influenced by the negative attitudes which surround you. Consciously change the Habits which are not life-enhancing - these include physical, mental, emotional and spiritual Habits - starting with those which are most obvious to you. There will be internal conflict because the personality has been driven by these props for as long as it can remember, but this is where your Constructive Thinking, Imagination, Prayer, and Faith must come into play. Fight the battle and crush your fear based Habits, just as Jean D'Arc crushed the English. Remember, her fellow Frenchmen fought for one hundred years and saw nothing but defeat. She fought for less than one year and reclaimed the throne."

I know what he is telling me and fully understand his analogy. There are many Habits which I say I will stop one day, but not today. Most of these Habits though are physical Habits. Daryl mentioned mental, emotional, spiritual *and* physical Habits. I wonder what the difference is and how I can tell whether I have fear based Habits in these different areas.

"Other people have questioned the same thing," he says, reading my mind again. "Mental Habits we have already talked about in lesson number three: they are associated with the way we think and how we can eliminate detrimental thought patterns. If you commence the process of changing your thoughts you will naturally change some of your emotional, physical, and even spiritual Habits."

I nod in agreement. When I am feeling down because I *think* I am failing at life, my first reaction is to go out and consume alcohol (which I assume is a physical Habit) or to feel anger and frustration at those around me (which in turn is an emotional Habit).

"Emotional Habits can be seen in the way you react to people and circumstances. If a person is thrown off centre by something which happens or things don't go to plan and they automatically fall into a default emotion, such as fear, anxiety, sadness and even anger, then this is an emotional Habit. They are automatic responses which are based on past experiences and conditioning, and they persist even when there's no logical reason to feel that way. If you wake up feeling good, then it's a good day; if you're feeling anxious, then you tend to feel precarious all day. While it's great to be in touch with your feelings, Emotional Habits can lead you down the wrong path."

"And these are connected to the way I think," I conclude loudly, recalling the continued fear I used to feel when Francois was talking to other females.

"That depends on the most obvious aspect of whether there is any *need* to feel fear, anger, anxiety, etc by the situation posed. If the answer is 'yes' you simply look at what you can do about it, and if the answer is 'no' then you need to start looking at your thought patterns - your Mental Habits - because feelings are preceded by thoughts. Find out what your thoughts are saying to generate those feelings and there you have the root of your Emotional Habit. When you know this you can change your inner dialogue, using the methods of Constructive thinking and Visualization."

Without having to think too hard about this I am aware of my emotional Habits, and they are those relating to a lack of trust, the root being the fear of betrayal. I know I have spent many years looking at life through the eyes of mistrust - seeing deceit in almost every crack and crevice - and yet this is not a true reflection of life. Daryl has taught me that. I have simply been conditioned to look at life in this way and have never forced myself, or challenged myself, to look at it any differently. But now I can.

"Physical Habits may come in the form of addictions, or even much smaller traits as biting finger nails, anything which you use as a crutch to help you feel secure, happy and in control, for a short time at least. However, it is easy to see that these Habits are linked to emotional needs, and therefore a physical Habit which is not life-enhancing is usually a sign that there is something deeper which needs addressing, so we look in turn at the emotional connection and then the thought pattern behind it.

"This leads me onto Truth and the need for good spiritual Habits. The greatest spiritual law which governs all other laws is that of Truth. Man does not need learned knowledge and certificates of success to know the difference between Truth and non-Truth. His first responsibility is to be true to himself: to not lie to himself or to others. Deceit and lies are the traps which ensnare good men. Families break down and bonds are shattered when man embarks on the journey of deceit. If you find yourself making excuses for your behaviour or actions, it is certain that you are not acting from Truth. You could rationalize and view situations from many angles, but Truth will always shout the loudest. If you choose to ignore this, you are essentially deceiving yourself, another fear based Habit."

This last comment about Truth causes me to think again of Francois. I am aware he occupies a substantial amount of my mental capacity, perhaps because of the effect he had on my life. This in itself has become a Habit. During our relationship I developed many Habits relating to him, and because I chose to ignore the Truth of the situation, I sunk deeper into feelings of despair.

First of all there was the element of trust: because he cheated on me, and lied to me, I did not believe many things he said. I did not trust him. Because I did not trust him, I found myself questioning his actions and hence developed the emotional Habit of interrogation to alleviate fears of betrayal during our relationship. Many times I wanted to walk away from him, to pack my bags and go, but I was afraid. I felt that I needed him in my life. Or rather I convinced myself that I needed him even though my insides were shattered, so perhaps this was both an emotional and a mental Habit. To mask my inner feelings, I developed the physical Habit of smoking marijuana daily, to the extent that my nerves were frayed if I had to go twenty-four hours without any. This then became the Habit that bonded Francois and I since we both felt relaxed in each other's company when in this intoxicated state. When I made the effort to break this Habit of smoking, he would not entertain the notion and so my attempts were short lived. Only when I decided to face the Truth of the matter that I did not trust Francois and that a successful relationship cannot be built on such a foundation was I able to smile again. Even now I am able to recall the wonderful feeling of liberation when I finally packed my belongings and left.

"And this leads me onto Love," smiles Daryl. "No matter what you may want to feel, you must adopt the spiritual Habit of projecting only love, because love conquers all. There is no feeling greater than love, and it must start by loving G.O.D. with your whole heart. If you love G.O.D. with your whole heart you will give yourself fully over to His service and hence your destiny. Next, you must love your fellow man, be it a friend, enemy, stranger or family member. If a person wrongs you, then love him. If somebody hurts you, love him. Seek only to love, and you will begin to experience the beauty that is stored within life. Do not feel guilty about believing in a love so strong and deep that it is invincible, because it exists in the format you believe it to."

"Sometimes I think I fall in love too easily," I find myself saying. "Is this a good or bad Habit?"

"It depends on what your driving force is. If you fall in love because you need companionship to make you feel confident about yourself, then this is a fear based Habit and is an emotional bind. To truly love there are no strings attached. Love is not about monitoring a persons' every move, or seeking to control them out of fear. Love is a feeling that liberates and encourages you to be greater than what you are at present. Do not confuse Love with needy emotions."

"You have spoken about many things to me today and I wonder if I will be able to remember everything you have said. There has been a lot to take in over the past six days."

"You will, but do not rely solely on memory. Use the power of Prayer."

Daryl looks at his watch. I notice we have been sat in the Market Square for almost two hours. Time passes quickly when I am in his company and I find myself wishing he would live locally so I could see him daily.

"Make G.O.D. your Habit Jane and He will give you everything you need. I am just His messenger, here to serve His purpose. Your role is the same, but you must take heed of what we have shared over this past week. Spend the rest of the day thinking about what we have discussed so far. Tomorrow is our last day and the topic is Intuition. Think about it and what it means, and do not be afraid to act on Intuition in the meantime."

I bid him farewell and watch as he walks away. The Market Square is busy with people rushing around like ants on a unified task of gathering. It is lunchtime so there is a dash to fill the half-hour break that has been allocated from the work place. My thoughts turn to the college: Jim will be stood in line at the canteen, Derek will be popping one of the twenty-three tablets he needs to take daily, and Graham will be sat eating his cheese and onion brown bread sandwich. They have done the same thing every day for as long as I have known them.

***

"Hello mum.."

"Jane, is that you?"

"Yes."

"Oh Jane, I have been so worried about you. I have hardly slept a wink. You know I worry about you, and you did not reply to the message I left you. You know how it makes me feel when I have not spoken to you in a while."

"It has only been a couple of days, and besides I have been busy."

"Oh, you have been back at work? That's good. I knew you would see sense love. Don't give that job up."

"Look mum, I haven't been back to work, and to be honest I don't know if I am going to go back. A lot has happened to me this last week, and it is causing me to question a few things."

"Like what love?"

"About my life, and what I am doing, where I am going, that sort of stuff."

"What has brought this about?"

"Remember last week, I told you I met a man in a café?"

"Oh, don't tell me you met with him again. He has not convinced you to join some sort of religious order has he? I told you to be on your guard, because you know that............."

As I listen to mother, I realize just how set in her ways she is. She has her view of things and that is how it will stay. To change her opinion of me and the boundaries of our relationship, I need to be confident in *my* beliefs and who *I am*. If I lack this confidence, this knowing in my own character, then people will fail to have confidence in me also. For several years now I have allowed mother to confuse my thoughts: this is no fault of hers, but is a weakness of mine. When I imagined her letting go of the chain, she herself said that I had put the chains on myself. She was only reacting to me in this way because they were the ground rules we had established between ourselves.

"Look mum," I interrupt. "I want you to listen for a moment, and to try and understand me. Something has changed in me over these past few days and I need to spend some time alone. I am not going to phone you for a while because I need to hibernate for a bit, spend some time getting to know myself again."

Silence follows, and then her response surprises me. "I understand love. I went through a similar experience when I was younger, so I know how you are feeling, and even though I will worry about you I won't contact you until you feel ready OK."

Tears roll down my cheeks and I suddenly feel guilty for wanting to draw back from her for a while, then I hear the voice that says it is OK, do what you feel is right.

"I love you mum," I say.

"I know you do. Perhaps you could write to me instead, only if you feel like it. I know how much you like writing. Only the other day I was telling a woman at the bus stop how much you like writing."

"Ok mum, I might do that."

INTUITION

Few are those who see with their own eyes and feel with their own hearts

Einstein

The preparations for my final meeting with Daryl feel almost ceremonious. I decide to dress well as a mark of respect and to prepare him a gift as my way of saying thank you.

My thoughts turn to Mick and how his body will be stone cold. This time last week he was alive and enjoying his memories of a good weekend. Now he is dead and enjoying nothing. What would he have done differently if he knew his time was up? Would it have made a difference to him? Did he live the life he wanted and so was ready to go at that moment in time?

How would I be different if I knew I had but twenty-four hours to go? Many people say you should live each day as if it is your last, but if this was the last day for me it would be such a crying shame. I have not done what I would love to do. Up until this point I have been quite cowardly, waiting for life to force me into situations rather than going with feelings and Intuition which tell me where I need to go and what I need to do. In the past I have completely ignored the inner call of my Spirit and instead based my actions on the many excuses and alternative options I could find.

Intuition told me to leave Francois four years earlier than what I did. I ignored it, and paid the price.

Intuition told me to embark on A-levels of my choice. I ignored it, listened to others, and paid the price.

Intuition has spoken to me many times, but I ignored it, and each time paid the price.

It is a well known fact that when certain organs or muscles in the body are not used they atrophy, the message to the brain being that they are no longer required by their user. Is this the same with Intuition? Could it simply waste away because it is ignored and not used for the purpose for what it is given?

***

"You ask a very valid question Jane, and the answer is yes. Intuition is the sensory organ of the Spirit and serves an essential role in the unfolding of mans unique destiny, his Life Plan. Do you know about the flight or fight syndrome?"

"Yes. I studied it briefly in biology and have experienced it myself a few times. It is a state that the body enters when it finds itself in a dangerous or fearful situation, asking itself whether it should stay and face the threat, or flee away from it," I reply.

"The flight or fight syndrome is one of the most common examples of Intuition, but it also works on very subtle levels. Sometimes it is a feeling of knowing, or it may be an urge to do something, for example taking an alternative route or visiting a specific place, or making a phone call. There are loads of ways Intuition works, and the key is to not ignore it but to *act* on it. It is this action which ensures your Life Plan unfolds as programmed by G.O.D."

I have met many people in my life who have told me that they ignored their Intuition. Only last week mother told me about a strong feeling she had to place a bet on the prospect of Manchester securing the bid to host the next Olympic Games, but she chose to ignore this because she feared the loss of money. If she had trusted her Intuition she would have been over sixteen thousand pounds better off. Mother is always talking about her need for more money and so spent several days mentally beating herself up for not placing the bet.

There are daily stories of people who have listened to their Intuition and have avoided death. When the Twin Towers in New York were destroyed by terrorists, several people reported that they had strong feelings about avoiding the workplace on that day.

But Intuition doesn't just involve events. A person may see another person for the first time and immediately know that there is a connection. Months later, they meet and a lasting friendship blossoms. There is the knowing that people have when they meet their life partner, with many confirming that they knew the first time they saw the other person that they would spend their lives together.

I ask Daryl why we choose to ignore our Intuition if it is such a valid tool. He replies that we live at a time in the world where science prevails and, because Intuition has not yet been fully analysed and understood by scientific bodies, we do not give it the full validity it deserves. It is seen as a new-age phenomena even though it is as old as the Earth.

"People don't realize," he continues, "that to ignore Intuition is a choice that tells it *I don't need you. Your input is not necessary.* This leads to Intuition becoming a quiet voice until it eventually stops speaking all together. Many times man does not realize the great power he has within him. Intuition is G.O.D.s voice and by listening to it mistakes will never be made and all of life will be successful. How many times have you had a feeling to walk, say, a different way?"

"Many times, and usually when I go with the feeling I end up seeing somebody I know and have not seen in a long time. More often than not the person in question has been thinking of me," I tell Daryl.

"If man was truly a being of Intuition, he would never need to worry about what the future held. He would not waste his time thinking about possible events years down the line because he would be focused on every moment, listening to Intuition and reacting to it. Intuition is not a learned trait: it is given to man at birth and is part of the True-Self. What it becomes though is an idle asset as the Ego-Self chooses to ignore it."

"How does a person learn how to use Intuition?" I ask, intrigued.

"You simply learn by *doing*. Every time you listen and act on Intuition you give it power. The more you act, the more natural it becomes until it is a Habit. Have Faith that Intuition knows what is the very best for you, even if your man-made logic tries to tell you different. Constructive thinking and Prayer are also essential here. The majority of people argue with Intuition until they convince themselves there is no need to act. Constructive thinking will encourage you to work with Intuition, and Faith will give you the confidence to accept its direction; Prayer will remind you that you are being guided by G.O.D. and will give you the guarantee that, each time you act upon Intuition, you are one step closer towards fulfilling your destiny."

"You have a Habit of making everything sound so interesting and easy! In theory everything you have taught me seems like a walk in the park, but I think all these methods I am to start adopting will be much harder in reality."

"You have responded with a Destructive thought. Resist these, because they will hinder your progress. Continued effort is necessary but do not see it as difficult: view it as an adventure, a journey, which only *you* can take. In situations such as these you really have nothing to lose and if you find yourself losing heart then ask yourself the simple question: Am I happy with the way my life is now, in the situations I choose to abide in? If the answer is no, keep seeking to change yourself until you can answer yes."

I draw a deep breath and take in the information Daryl has just given me. He watches me with his blue eyes, twinkling like diamonds from a face that is clothed in serenity. He carries with him, at all times, a sense of joy. He is somebody who is clearly happy to be where he is at, doing what he loves. I take the opportunity to ask him again about his background.

"Now that we are coming to the end of the lessons, I am happy to share with you some of my personal history. If I had told you at the start of our meetings you would not have returned to me because your Habit of judging others would have caused you to ignore what I had to offer. But now I feel you can listen without prejudice.

In short, my father placed me in a psychiatric hospital at the age of fourteen because he felt I was unruly but, in reality, I was merely a boy who was adventurous and questioned much of what I saw around me. Today people would say I was a victim of the system. The more I fought for my sanity and freedom, the more I was classed as being mentally disturbed, and various treatments were imposed upon me. I even think I became a guinea pig for some of the new, trendy, psychiatric treatments which various doctors and pharmaceutical companies promoted.

I spent thirty-five years being treated for mental illness, four of which were confined to a high level security room. In this time my only solace was reading and I eventually discovered this book: Universal Intelligence. This became my confident and friend and, by changing my outlook and thoughts on the situation, I was able to gain my freedom - a freedom harnessed first through the Spirit and then physically.

Man does not realise that in his daily Habits he is more of a prisoner than what I was. He willingly places himself in a cell and spends his entire life there. Only a few dare to seek the life that eats away at their insides."

I am surprised by Daryl's revelations but feel strengthened by them. It shows me that I am in a much healthier position than what he was to make effective change in my life. It is only my choices which confine me, and the door to my cell has always been open. I imagine in Daryl's case this was not always so. Until a person of professional rank signed his discharge papers he was still at the mercy of the institution and the orders of doctors. At any moment in time I can go anywhere and do anything. It is all down to me and how I decide to act. What am I waiting for? Why have I spent the past few years wearing a straightjacket in a mental cell, wallowing in a psychological cesspit that I created myself?

G.O.D. has given me a destiny, a unique Life Plan which is mine and mine alone. He has given me powerful tools to use, and yet what have I done with them? I have ignored them all, preferring instead to live a life that other people live - lives which seem to leave them unfulfilled and cynical. How can I proclaim to have a brain when I cannot even use its basic functions? Why do I sit daydreaming of the treasures of better days when I can reach out for them now?

"You are everything you ever dream about and much more Jane. People will force their opinions on you, but only take those which resonate with Truth. Everything else is a decoy. Be special and spread good works. Now you know the gifts I have shared with you over this past week you must use them and, more importantly, tell others about them. Continually refine your thoughts and Habits; Pray and have Faith; trust and always seek the Truth. And finally, allow Intuition her voice. She has your best interests at heart."

A tear comes to my eye when I see Daryl stand and lift his coat off the back of the chair. "Before I go I would like to give you this," he says.

He takes a book out of his coat pocket and hands it to me. It is a copy of Universal Intelligence. I open it and see an inscription he has written:

Wisdom is more valuable than gold and can save the life of a man. It will be a great friend to you on your journey.

I wipe the tear from my eye and reply that I have something for him, to say thank-you for the time he has given me.

I hand him a small parcel and he asks if I would like him to open it now. I tell him it is his choice. He slowly peels back the wrapping paper to unveil a photo frame.

"What is this?" he asks.

"It is a passage that I wrote for you. I wanted to sum up everything you have taught me and give you something to take away with you. I see you as a friend Daryl, and my life is going to be a much better experience because of your willingness to teach me. It is my way of saying thank you, and to let you know that I understand what you have taught me."

Daryl puts his glasses on and reads the passage aloud:

To every man there opens a way,
And the high soul climbs the higher way,
And the low soul gropes the low;
And in between on the misty flats,
The rest drift to and fro.
But to every man there opens
A high way and a low,
And every man decides
The way his soul shall go

***

As I pass the Statue I notice that something has changed about her and I am sure I just saw her glance at me from beneath her brow. This brings a smile to my face and a feeling comes over me as though I am not going to be seeing her for a while.

The poster in the travel agents window calls out to me again, the difference being that I am now ready to respond. Confidently I walk towards the holiday shop, all the time my eyes fixed on the colourful poster. As I enter a lady sitting behind a desk asks if she can help me. Pointing to the window I tell her I would like to go to the destination on the poster.

"That's not such a good idea," she replies with a friendly smile. "You see, there have been reports of hurricanes in that part of the world."

"Oh, I had set my sights on going there. I have even pictured myself on *that* beach."

"So, it is a beach holiday you're after is it?" I nod. "Well, let me see what I have got on the system."

I sit down and the assistant starts typing fast on a keyboard. Nerves try to tie my stomach up in knots but my mind won't allow it. Does it feel right to be sat here? Yes, it does. Is this what I want to be doing? Yes it is, I affirm. Well then, I tell myself, no arguments, no nerves, just enjoy this moment and all will be fine.

After several minutes the travel agent tells me she has a flight leaving for Phi Phi Island the next day.

"Phi Phil Island?" I ask. "Where is that?"

"Thailand."

I pause for a moment. "Thailand, I have always wanted to go there."

"Would you like to see some pictures?"

The travel agent turns the computer screen at an angle so we can both see the display. The first picture she shows me is of a long boat sailing through a narrow gorge. It sits serenely on a gentle turquoise stretch of water, bordered on both sides by imposing rock faces. The sky is bright blue with fine wisps of white cloud. It is stunning. For a moment I see myself sat on the boat, soaking up the tranquility of the surroundings. It feels good.

The second picture is of a swimming pool. "This is your hotel," she says.

It is beautiful. A line of large, double sized sun loungers face an emerald green pool. Palm trees and tropical plants surround the area, casting shadows onto the water. It looks like a manmade oasis in the middle of a tropical jungle: a hidden treasure that only the ardent traveler will discover. I imagine relaxing on a sun lounger, wearing sunglasses and writing on a notepad.

"And this," she says showing another picture, "is the beach."

"I am sold," I say. "I will take the next available flight."

***

I cross the Market Square and give the Statue a final look. The sun comes out from behind a cloud and shines brightly upon her face. For the first time I see a look of elation in her eyes, an emotion I have not seen before. I walk over to her and touch her back, a gesture which symbolises respect and gratitude for her devotion and service to me.

As I stand at her side I hear Daryl's voice loud and clear, but I do not see him. 'Well done Jane. You have picked more than a destination: you have chosen your destiny. You will take many journeys from here on and will document them in your own words, and these will become essential guides for others to use. This is your Call and your real work has now begun. Enjoy it.'

About the Author

Joanne St.Clair is a qualified teacher who holds an Honors Degree in Aerospace Engineering. She has fifteen years of experience as an engineering lecturer in Further and Higher Education, as well as expertise of business and financial management within the music industry.

For the past twelve years she has been a disciplined student of the Spiritual Laws which govern and underpin all of Life, and her on-going passion and enthusiasm in this field has led her to Holisitic Counselling, Reiki, Metaphysics, New Thought Principles, Christian Science, and Meditation and Visualisation Techniques.

Joanne has a deep seated passion to inspire, educate, empower and motivate people to use the incredible power of their thoughts; to understand the great force of their subconscious mind; and to fully utilize the amazing gift of prayer and feeling in everyday life.

Joanne currently lives in Lancashire with her husband Daniel and their two children, Elijah and Amelia. Together they continue to promote the use of Spiritual Laws to achieve success and prosperity in life and business.

Recommended Authors

Neville Goddard
Norman Vincent Peale
Catherine Ponder
Dale Carnegie
Napolean Hill
Morris Goodman
Rhonda Byrne
Emma Curtis Hopkins
Wallace D Wattles
James Allen

Recommended viewing

Rev Ike
The Secret

Made in the USA
Lexington, KY
07 May 2012